SEASONS OF
LIFE

Bobby & Ronnie,

I hope you enjoy reading this and I pray that God blesses you and your family!

Love,
M.J. Sch...

SEASONS OF LIFE
AUTUMN'S CHANGES

M. J. SCHEETS

TATE PUBLISHING
AND ENTERPRISES, LLC

Seasons of Life
Copyright © 2014 by M. J. Scheets. All rights reserved.

No part of this publication may be reproduced, stored in a retrieval system or transmitted in any way by any means, electronic, mechanical, photocopy, recording or otherwise without the prior permission of the author except as provided by USA copyright law.

This novel is a work of fiction. Names, descriptions, entities, and incidents included in the story are products of the author's imagination. Any resemblance to actual persons, events, and entities is entirely coincidental.

The opinions expressed by the author are not necessarily those of Tate Publishing, LLC.

Published by Tate Publishing & Enterprises, LLC
127 E. Trade Center Terrace | Mustang, Oklahoma 73064 USA
1.888.361.9473 | www.tatepublishing.com

Tate Publishing is committed to excellence in the publishing industry. The company reflects the philosophy established by the founders, based on Psalm 68:11,
"The Lord gave the word and great was the company of those who published it."

Book design copyright © 2014 by Tate Publishing, LLC. All rights reserved.
Cover design by Carlo nino Suico
Interior design by Jomel Pepito

Published in the United States of America

ISBN: 978-1-63122-818-6
Fiction / Christian / General
14.04.09

This book is dedicated to my Lord, God, and Savior. He told me to write, and I did. He is my way, my truth, my life, and my best friend. Thanks for never leaving my side. I will forever serve you!

CHAPTER 1

Autumn sat on the back of her sister's red Chevy, the breeze tossing her silky, black hair. Sonic's parking lot was crowded at this time of day. In the small town of Hickory, there wasn't a lot to do, so everyone seemed to gather there. But Autumn didn't mind living in a small town, in fact she preferred it. And with summer break nearing its end, Autumn and her other adopted siblings finally were able to get together. It seemed to Autumn that it was getting harder and harder for their family to stay in touch, let alone make time to hang out. Their parents Kent and Lori Snow couldn't have kids of their own, so they took it as a rare blessing from God and decided to adopt. They grasped the opportunity to love some of God's children that had been turned away from the people that were entrusted with their care.

Autumn looked at Winter, the first of the five to be adopted. Kent and Lori adopted her at birth. Winter, being a botched abortion, was very lucky, considering her birth mother tried to end the pregnancy on several occasions before she was put in touch with Kent and Lori. God had protected her in the womb for when she was born, she was perfectly healthy aside from being underweight. Today, she had tight golden ringlets that made all of the other girls just a little jealous. Her eyes were a very light shade of brown that would brighten and sparkle when she laughed. She was considered the beauty of the family. At the moment, she was smiling, as always, at their brother, Garret, who was telling the girls one of his wild tales, as usual.

Autumn and her cousins Summer and Garret were adopted into the family when Winter was two. They were found locked in a closet, half starved, dehydrated, and abandoned by their only living relative, Autumn's real father. All three cousins had great a resemblance to each other. All had black hair. Summer and Garret both had blue eyes, but Autumn had green.

Autumn glanced over at Spring, the last to be adopted. She was sitting in the back of Summer's truck, not really joining in with the rest of them and was messing with her phone, like always. Spring was adopted when she was four. No one knew her story. She never would tell and would get all mad and defensive if asked. Kent and Lori was understanding and kept her secret. It took almost a year for Spring to relax enough to trust the family.

Autumn let out a sigh. Life was easier for everyone after Spring got settled in, but now it seemed that within the last two years, she started reverting back to the recoiled, untrusting, quiet sister. A play punch to her shoulder awoke Autumn from her reminiscing.

"Hey, Autumn, why so gloom? Are you starting to take after Spring?" Garret's playful smile didn't help his joke. Spring's glare spoke volumes.

"If you call me that one more time—"

Garret threw his hands up. "Sorry! Sorry! Gees, Spree, it was just a joke!"

Kent and Lori had a since of humor. Having already named Winter and all four girls being around the same age, they grasped the opportunity, leaving Garret the only one with a normal name. Spring was the only one who actually cared but claimed that the new name was better than her last.

Autumn smiled and answered her brother's question, "It's just sad that we won't be able to get together like this for a while. With everyone gone to different places during the school year, it's hard to enjoy college without some annoying little brother bugging you all the time." She smiled at her own joke. Garret, not missing a beat, replied, "Aw, sis, I didn't know you cared!" He wrapped his arm around her and proceeded to mess up her hair, which resulted in them getting into a wrestling match on the truck bed. Spring hollered for them to stop when they smashed her feet.

Summer rolled her eyes. "You two are so immature!" Garret's phone rang, breaking up the scuffle.

"We'll finish this later!" he whispered before he answered the phone.

"Garret Tyler Storm. Garret speaking. How may I direct you call?" They all rolled their eyes at him as a long pause proceeded and he hung up his phone.

"Okay. Mom and dad has a surprise for us, says to come home." They all scrambled off the truck to leave.

"Hey, tell Kent and Lori I'll be back later." They all stared at Spring in disbelief.

"Spree, why?" Winter said. Spring huffed as she rolled her eyes. "I'm going to see Rob, okay? Do I have to inform you of everything I decide to do?" Winter spoke up in the gentle tone that she had, "Well, maybe you could come back with us for a little while and then see him before you leave to go back to college." Spring let out a sigh. "Fine." Then she climbed into her car and left. Without offering to give anyone a ride back, she left the remaining four to cram themselves into Summer's truck.

Autumn and her siblings finally made it home. Autumn ended up having to sit on Garret's lap, but it could have been worse. When Summer pulled her truck to a stop beside Spring's car, Garret threw open the truck door, dumping Autumn on the ground. He howled with laughter. Autumn jumped up and yanked him out, tripping him at the same time. She smiled as he fell on his face.

"Pay back hurts doesn't it little brother?" Autumn replied. He rolled over and smiled at her.

"Why yes it does. So now that you have broken every bone in my body, you can carry me into the house." Autumn burst into laughter as she walked past him.

When they entered the house, the smell of delicious food filled their noses. Their mom, Lori, smiled back at them.

"Surprise! I have made everyone's favorite foods!" Lori led them to the table and said grace. Autumn filled her plate as she said, "This is awesome! I'm starving." Kent raised an eyebrow.

"Really. Didn't you all just come from Sonic?" Autumn smiled and replied, "Well, yes. But we didn't exactly eat. We just had shakes and ice cream." Kent shook his head at her response.

"Oh, okay. Ice cream and milk shakes isn't enough to fill young adults. I get it now." Kent replied. Garret smiled at his dad.

"Yep, this is awesome! Are you going to do this every year when I have to go back to college?" A bit of Garret's food fell from his mouth as he spoke.

"Garret, don't talk with your mouth full." Replied Lori, "And I don't know, I might. Oh, and I don't know what I will do will all of you gone off to college." Autumn smiled as she said, "Well, Garret's not actually leaving. His welding tech school is just in the next town." Garret smiled in response.

"Yeah. I'm not leaving." At this point Summer spoke up, aggravation thick in her voice.

"Speaking of leaving… Thanks Spree for not offering to drive anyone home. It was interesting to try to fit everyone in my little truck." Spring just shrugged and said, "Whatever." Then she stood up and without looking at anyone, put her dishes in the sink. "Well, I'm going off to see Rob." Summer raised an eyebrow and she gathered everyone's plates as she asked, "But what about our plans?" Spring shrugged her shoulders again and replied, "I know we had plans, but Rob called at Sonic remember? And you might as well just go on to our dorm without me." Spring glanced at Summer's aggravated expression and then looked away.

"Hey! Don't get mad at me! I told him we had plans but… well anyway I don't want to upset him." Kent looked at Spring and said, "You know if he doesn't want you to spend time with your family then this is not a healthy relationship at all. And from what I've seen, he doesn't respect your dignity at all. In fact I think you both need to repent." Everyone was silent as they watched Spring's face redden.

"Shut up! Just shut up! You don't have a clue to what you are saying! Rob's a nice guy and I love him so stop pestering me about him." Spring shouted as she crammed stuff into her over night bag. Autumn glanced at Garret and Winter. They knew what was coming next so they excused themselves.

"I'm going to… uh… go… um… play some baseball with some friends." Garret announced as he hurried out the door.

"Yah, and I'm going to go pack." Replied Autumn. Winter nodded and said, "Yep, I had better go pack too." Autumn and Winter turned to go to their rooms. Autumn expected to hear Summer excuse herself too but what Summer actually said stopped both Autumn and Winter in their tracks.

"Mom and dad are right." Spring's mouth dropped open. "What!" Summer cleared her throat and repeated herself.

"I said mom and dad are right. You are just making yourself miserable. He doesn't care about you! All he wants you for is sex." Autumn and Winter looked at each other and hurried to their rooms as the sound of Spring cussing followed them. Autumn shut her door and tried not to hear the argument. She loved her sister and wanted her to be happy but she couldn't talk to her. Any time someone tried, it always ended in a fight.

Autumn packed as slowly as possible to try to wait it out the fight. She didn't want to get dragged into it like she had in the past. Only when she finally heard the door slam did she tip-toe back into the living room. Lori sat on the couch crying. She looked up as she heard Autumn enter the room.

"Hey sweetie. You all ready to visit Frank?" She asked softly. With the argument earlier Autumn had almost forgot about visiting her real dad in Miles City. She had spoke with Frank on several occasions through the phone and he had visited her a few times, but this was going to be the first time she would stay at his place for a few days. She wasn't sure how to feel about it. Frank was nice and they talked easily with each other, but she was still nervous about going to see him. *I can do this.* She told herself.

"Yah, I'm ready. I even got the directions." She said out loud. Winter walked into the room with and arm full of bedding.

"Well then I guess I will go get our dorm ready and I'll see you in three days." Winter said to Autumn as she went outside to put the bedding in her car. Autumn smiled and nodded to winter and then kissed her mom on the cheek.

"Okay then. I guess I'll see you all in a few weeks." Autumn said as she hugged Kent, fetched her things, and headed out the door.

Autumn pulled into the drive of her father's house. It was placed in a little run-down neighborhood where dogs barked constantly and the windows on all the houses were covered with either a blanket, heavy curtains, or something else that would keep people from seeing into the personal lives of those who covered it. The cold, unfriendly, suspicious feeling that she got about the place was even more confirmed by the bars on all the windows and doors. The yards were cluttered and overgrown, neglected and left to overtake the home. She pulled up to the garage that was attached to the house. Her dad, who had been looking for her, opened the door so she could pull her car in next to his. *Well*, she thought to herself, *Miles City would be hard to get used to.* Her heart already yearned for the stars and the wide open fields that were now hidden from her by the concrete jungle and the smoggy haze that filled the sky. She longed to hear the sweet sound of the crickets singing, the soft sound of the breeze drifting by, and the gentle murmur of cattle that had lull her to sleep in the past. But as it seemed, for tonight and maybe a few more, she would have to settle for the sound of sirens, cars, and the train that would pass by the house from three hundred feet away. Her country heart sank. But she forced a smile on her face for her father's sake. The smile on his was so huge that it almost seemed to cut his face in half.

After shutting the garage door and locking all three locks, her dad helped her get her stuff into the house. *So much for feeling safe!* She thought to herself. Back home, they hardly ever locked the door, let alone having three different locks on it. Her dad gave her a hug that was awkward for both of them.

"I am so glad that you are here! Let me show you to your room." Her dad took her hand and proceeded to lead her down the hall.

"Fra—I mean Dad, you do know that I can't stay here every weekend, right?" He shuffled his feet and looked at her with his cool gray eyes that peeked through the mass of black and gray hair.

"Yeah, I know. I also know that I will be leaving to work out west soon and won't get to see you for three years. So I guess I just wanted everything to be perfect since you've given me a second chance to be somewhat of the father that I should have been." Speechless, Autumn just smiled and laid her overnight bag on the bed and followed him to the kitchen to eat.

The pizza reminded Autumn of how hungry she was. But as she ate, she couldn't help but think about what he said. How could her own flesh and blood become so insane as to lock her and two other kids in a closet and leave them to die? Was he sorry for what he did? She opened her mouth to ask, but fear caught fire in her heart. Instead, she took another bite of pizza and listened to her father excitedly tell her how his life had gotten so much better after asking Jesus Christ back into his life. This was just the first day; why spoil it with the past? There would be another time.

CHAPTER 2

Spring pulled into her boyfriend's driveway. Her emotions were in an uproar after the argument with Kent and Lori, even Summer! Summer had actually entered the much-fought-over topic and had taken their side. She sat in her car, waiting for Robert to come out; of course, he didn't. Sighing, she climbed out and entered his house. As usual, he was sitting on the couch with a beer in his hand. But this time, he was on the phone. He jumped when she walked in.

"I gotta go. I'll talk to ya later. Bye." He snapped the phone shut as she grabbed a soda out of the fridge.

"Who was that?" she asked. "Oh, no one. Just an old friend." He got up and wrapped his arms around her, grabbing her butt in the process.

"Man, I'm glad you're here. What took you so long?" Without waiting for a reply, he proceeded to kiss her neck and let his hands drift. She pushed him away. Frowning, he almost yelled, "What's wrong with you?"

"I had another fight with Kent and Lori today. They had some surprise dinner where they made all of our favorite foods. So I was polite and stayed for a little bit. When I went to leave, the fight started. They said that what we're doing is wrong and we need to repent of our sins."

"So forget them!" He moved toward her again. She stepped back, ignoring the aggravated look on his face.

"But this time, Summer joined in on the fight, and she said that I am poisoning myself and one day, I'll regret it. Oh! And she said that you're trash and all you want me for is sex!" There was silence. She stood there, staring at her soda, afraid to see his face. Afraid to see the look that would confirm what Summer had said. He yanked her into his arms, and with that smoldering look that she usually liked, he replied, "Spree, you know I love you. You are an adult, and they're not your real parents anyway, so forget about them. Forget about everyone, even your stupid sister or whatever she is to you. It's just me and you now." His expression turned to hunger as he forcefully put her mouth to his. For a brief second, what her sister had told her returned. *He doesn't care about you or how you feel. Just watch, when you run into his arms today to tell him how horrible we all are, will he sit and listen, or will he just blow you off? When he kisses you, will he do it with respect and honor you, or will he do it with a possessive manner, not caring if it hurts?* Spring had run out of the house at that point not wanting to hear more. "You'll regret it someday!" had followed her out the door and all the way to his house, and her sister's words cut to the bone.

For a minute, she realized that her sister was right about Rob. But the sudden panic was soon replaced by prideful anger. *Who are they to tell me what I shouldn't do? Or what is right and wrong?* She kissed him back with force. He jumped on it, grabbing at her clothes to remove them. Startled but still driven by anger, she didn't stop him and let herself be surrendered to the beast called lust. *They all said the devil would get my soul. Well, let him. I'm going to make my own choices from now on*, Spring decided.

CHAPTER 3

Summer drove her old red Chevy down the interstate. She was fuming as well but in a different way. Her heart ached for her sister Spring. Like the rest of the sisters, she had kept her mouth shut when Spring got into a fight with their mom and dad. But this time, she took her parents' side. She didn't want Spring to be hurt by Robert any more. *Why couldn't she see that he didn't love her at all? All he wanted was her body. It was plain as day!* At first, he had charmed her with gifts and dinner dates, but he would never come into the house to pick her up. He always waited in the car. He never came to Spring's birthday, to Christmas, or her graduation party. Even though Spring tried to hide it, everyone saw the hurt on her face. He always wanted her to go to his house, and she never got home before midnight. Two o'clock in the morning was early! And the more everyone tried to talk to her about it, the angrier and more rebellious she got. Summer rubbed her temple as she pulled into Casey's gas station in Booton. She and Spring had, had plans today. They were going to drive in one vehicle to save money and spend the remaining part of the day window shopping and decorating their dorm. But no, Robert called and told her to come to his place. When Spring told him that she had other plans, he got mad, so Spring went to his house instead. Anger boiled in Summer's chest. She pulled up to a pump, selected a fuel type, and started filling up.

So wrapped up in her thoughts, she didn't notice the blue Dodge that had pulled up to the pump next to her. A guy with brown hair and freckles wearing a green John Deere baseball cap climbed out and started pumping. Noticing how agitated she looked, he leaned against the side of his truck and smiled. "Howdy!"

Caught off guard, she jumped and turned to see who spoke. Nodding in his direction, she replied, "Hey." He ambled over to her, giving her truck the once-over.

"Nice ride! 95 Chevy. Good shape. Silverado! Powerful model! But of course, it could never outrun a Dodge!" He leaned against her truck this time, a little too close for her comfort. Summer took a step back and lifted an eyebrow. "Pardon me? Did you just ask for a race?"

He leaned closer to her. "No, ma'am, I would never ask a woman to bet against me when I know that there is absolutely no chance of her winning! How awful would I be to take advantage of a poor, defenseless woman driving a Chevy?" He winked at her as he walked back to his truck and replaced the gas nozzle.

"What? Are you afraid that I will look back and see you eating my dust?"

With that, he laughed, and as he walked toward the store to pay, he replied, "You wish!"

She shook her head as prideful anger now filled her heart. She finished pumping and swiped her debit card hard through the machine. *Who was he to say that I couldn't beat him in a race? He's just a smooth talking coward! A flirt too!* The gas pump beeped at her, rejecting her card. Confused, she swiped it again and then headed inside to pay after the machine refused her debit card the second time. She got to the door just as he was coming out. He handed her a scrap of paper. "Here's the number for the towing company. You might need it." A cocky smirk was plastered on his face.

She put her hands on her hips and smiled slightly. "Do you always try to attract girls this way or just me?" She made sure to put a little bite in her tone.

He leaned in close and whispered in her ear, "Just you." Backing off a bit to see her reddening face, he spoke again, "And who's trying?" With that, he turned away. Rolling her eyes, Summer walked to the counter. But before she could say anything, the smiling cashier said, "He already paid for it." Puzzled and secretly pleased, she got in her truck and left.

CHAPTER 4

Autumn paced the floor while she waited for Winter to show up. Winter's class was running late, and if she didn't hurry, they wouldn't make it. Autumn checked her watch and grimaced. Last semester, they had gotten into the habit of going to a cowboy church on the outside of town. It sang of home and love. She didn't want to miss it. Tuesdays only came once a week. The church held services on Tuesday so the rodeo folks could come and everyone else could go to other churches as well. After this year, she would have her associate's degree and would return back home. She knew that she would miss the church. The door flew open, bringing Autumn out of her thoughts. Winter rushed in, threw her stuff on her bed, and both girls ran out to the car.

Soon they were on the dirt road that led to the church. Dust filled the air, and they could barely see the vehicle in front of them. Eventually, the dust dispersed enough for them to see a clearing completely full of cars. They parked and followed some people who were making their way to the other side of the clearing. A fair-sized house appeared standing next to a very large barn-looking building. Horses stomped and neighed in a small round pen beside the building. As Autumn and Winter approached the building, they had to slide out of the way for three little boys that ran by them. Like the rest of the children, they were running toward the house where a middle-aged woman stood, beckoning them in. Autumn and Winter slid in the door of the church to find only two seats left. They unwillingly took the seats on opposite sides of the room. Winter, who was the first to enter, took the seat on the outside by a young couple. But Autumn had to slide past a rough-looking cowboy. He had his black felt hat sitting precariously on his lap along with a much-worn Bible. He was covered in dirt like he had just come straight in from the field with no time to shower and change. But like a gentleman, he stood up to let her squeeze past him. "Ma'am"

"Thank you," she replied. His voice was very masculine, rumbling deep in his chest. His shoulders were so broad that he was only an inch from her. She was close enough to feel the heat coming off his body. Autumn blushed slightly at herself. She shouldn't be noticing things like that. She didn't even know him. But it was hard not to notice the blond-haired cowboy sitting next to her. Taking a deep breath, she turned her attention to the sermon. As usual, the sermon hit home. The preacher, a heavyset fellow with

Seasons of Life

a handlebar mustache and a twinkle in his eye, wasn't the type to tiptoe around things; he was straightforward. But just as the preacher was getting ready for the closing prayer, the cowboy sitting next to her shifted a little, accidentally knocking his hat to the floor. Absentmindedly, she reached to pick it up for him. Their hands touched. She recoiled as she whispered an apology. After this, she found it hard to pay attention to the closing prayer or the announcement of refreshments at the back of the room. After everyone was released, Autumn stood to leave and turned to see the cowboy standing in her way, looking at her with his mysterious blue eyes. Her heart pounded in her chest.

"Howdy, ma'am, the name's Luke. Luke Buckner." She shook his hand and tried to calm herself before answering. He had a firm but tender grasp.

"Hi, Luke. I'm Autumn Leaves." His dazzling smile sent his turquoise-blue eyes sparkling.

"Nice to meet you. Interesting handle though." She smiled and had to laugh a little. She started to open her mouth to answer when she noticed movement to her left. She turned just in time to see a man with black hair, covered in dirt as well, leap over a row of chairs. His foot caught on one of them, and it clattered to the ground with a loud clang, quieting the room. All eyes were on him as the man leaped to his feet.

"Pardon me," he replied to the crowd before turning to face Winter. Breathing heavily, he stated, "Ma'am, I have been trying dearly to make your acquaintance, and I dare say that I have made a fool of myself trying to!" At that point, he whipped off his hat, bowed to her, and then smiled. The entire room erupted into laughter, and both Winter and the man's faces turned beet red. Luke shook his head and made his way to the man, with Autumn in tow. They weaved their way between chairs and people, occasionally being stopped to speak with someone Luke knew.

When they finally made it over, Winter and the man were deep in conversation. Luke stepped forward to introduce Autumn. "Autumn, this is Jacob Jackson."

Smiling, he shook her hand. "Ma'am, it's a pleasure to make your acquaintance on this fine evening and your friend here, especially your friend."

Winter blushed and Luke chuckled. "You have to excuse him. He's a romantic. Reads Shakespeare and such." Jacob frowned. "Beg your pardon! You of all people know why I talk like I do. I daresay I am not a romantic. This language is a dying art, and I shall uphold it!" Luke just smiled and shook his head. Jacob, ignoring his friend's silent reply, leaned toward Winter and whispered, "By chance, could I convince such a beauty to dine with such a rugged cowboy like myself?" Winter blushed again. "Sorry, but I hardly know you. I kind of have a rule about going somewhere with someone I don't know." He tipped his hat in a little bow and smiled. "Then perhaps another time." His brown eyes showed disappointment, but he said nothing as he took her hand, kissed it, and left. Luke also tipped his hat and bid them a good night. Autumn watched him as he walked over and started talking to Rick, the preacher.

Three more men asked Winter out to eat before they made it to their car. Autumn wasn't surprised. With Winter's beautiful blond hair, striking brown eyes, and perfect figure, she was every man's dream. But Autumn still couldn't help feeling like the ugly, tagalong sister. Not one of the three men even glanced at her while they were begging Winter to accept them. In fact, the only man that actually held a conversation with her was Luke and the pastor. Winter's voice broke her from her thoughts.

"So Autumn, how does pizza sound?" Winter asked as she navigated her car through a maze of vehicles and people. Autumn shrugged her feelings aside and replied to her sister about eating out.

"Yeah, that's fine." Autumn replied.

They sat down at Pizza Hut, talking about a little bit of everything. After the food came, each fell into their own thoughtful silence. Autumn's thoughts surprised her as they took a turn and fell on Luke. She smiled. Luke seemed nice. He had good manners and was polite but quiet. Didn't everyone warn you about the quiet ones? Wasn't they supposed to draw you in with all the secrets and mysteries that they held? Well, it was working. She was definitely interested.

Luke drove his old Chevy truck down the dirt road toward his house. He had a lot on his mind tonight as well. After leaving the church, his best friend pulled him aside into the shadows. "Wait!" was all that he had said. They both stood there and watched as the girl Jacob had asked out turned down one guy after another. When they finally got in the truck to leave, Jacob was smiling from ear to ear.

"Well, she's honest! Now is she taken?" A blank stare had crossed Luke's face as realization hit. "What are you talking about, and why are you driving my truck instead of me?" Jacob smiled, and his eyes had that look in them that told Luke that he was in for trouble.

"I dare say to follow her and win her heart!"

Luke turned toward his friend. "No! Oh no, you are not! We are not... Pull this truck over. I..." The stern look that Jacob gave him made him stop talking. He let out a groan as he put his face in his hands.

So they followed the girls to Pizza Hut, where they watched them eat. Luke's stomach growled with hunger as he turned to face Jacob.

"Hey Jake, I'm gonna go get us some fo—"

"Shhh!"

"But I'm hu—"

"Shhh!"

"Jake!"

"SHHH!" Groaning, Luke rubbed his temples as he listened to his stomach complain. *I can't believe this is happening! Jacob has completely lost his mind. Spying on girls, and watching them eat while we starve to death!* Luke's temper flared up a little more. *And he hijacked my truck!* Luke shook his head and tried to calm his-self down. *It's ok. The girls will finish eating soon and I will be able to go home and pretend that I had no part in this stupid stunt.* He looked into the restaurant window where the girls sat. It didn't seem like they talked much. He watched Autumn's face. She seemed to be deep in thought. Then she smiled. No one had said anything to her... *I wander what she was thinking about that made her smile.* Luke tore his gaze away from her when he realized that he was staring. *What am I doing? Oh no. I'm getting as bad as Jacob!* Luke leaned his head back and closed his eyes in an effort to make time pass quickly.

Finally, they followed the girls back to the college where Luke made Jacob sit in the passenger's seat. As Luke started to pull out of the college parking lot, Jacob reported, "I'm in love! She's beautiful, honest, and she stirs my soul!" Luke had frowned and replied, "No! You're not in love. You can't fall in love that fast. Lust maybe, but not love! You don't even know her! This is the stupidest thing you have ever done. Oh, and when is your truck gonna be fixed so you'll quit using mine for wild goose chases?" Luke watched as his friend's face change from blissful happiness to deep hurt. Jacob left out all fancy talk as he said, "Luke, you are my best friend, so I will forgive you for what you said, but if this was such a stupid idea, then why didn't you stop me? And why did you spend most the time staring at Winter's friend?" Luke couldn't respond, so Jacob continued, "The black-haired beauty does have a mysterious attractiveness to her. As your friend, I encourage you to involve yourself with her."

They rode in silence until they got to Jacob's house. "Hey, Jake, sorry for hurting you. I'm just worried about ya. And I still don't think it's a good idea to jump the gun so soon." Jacob smiled and punched him on the shoulder. "Yeah, I know."

Luke finally got to his own house. He pulled into his drive, parked his truck by the front door, and pondered what Jacob had said that night. He *had* been watching Autumn. He had also noticed her beauty. He normally didn't introduce himself and make conversation with girls, especially ones he didn't know. So why did he today? He shook his head in confusion and bit into the Hardies double cheese burger that he had bought before he took Jacob home. He sighed and opened his Bible to take his problems to God.

CHAPTER 5

To Spring, the semester was passing by fairly quickly. She would leave every weekend so she could see Robert. He had been acting weird lately. Today, he told her not to come over till tomorrow because he wasn't going to be home. So she went to visit her parents Kent and Lori. They had been begging her to come visit anyway. Big mistake. Well, it started out okay, but like usual, the conversation eventually drifted to Robert, and like usual, a big fight erupted. So she left. She didn't want family picking her life apart. *Who needs them anyway?* She thought.

Now she was driving toward Robert's house. She knew he wouldn't be there, but after driving around town for an hour and still not knowing where to go (and not wanting to drive back to school), she felt his house to be the only place to go. Besides, she knew where the key was hidden, and she would just surprise him when he came home. Satisfied with her decision, she pulled into his drive.

She hit her brakes. Robert's car was right in front of her. *He must have gotten home early*, she told herself. She parked her car and climbed out. Another car sat beside Robert's. Frowning, she walked in like usual, almost bumping into a very skimpy-dressed redhead.

"Oh! I'm sorry! You must be Spree. Rob has told me so much about you! I'm Carrie." Carrie turned to face Rob, who was now standing by the kitchen table.

"Thanks for helping me with my homework!" Then with a little giggle, she walked out the door. Spring stood there not knowing what to say. Robert put his arms around her, hands already starting to drift.

"Baby! I've missed you!"

She pushed him away. "I think I'm going to be sick!" She ran to the bathroom and shut the door behind her. Her head was spinning with confusion, and her heart hurt. She closed her eyes as she tried not to hurl. When she got her stomach under control again, she reached for the water glass that Rob usually kept on the counter, but something caught her eye, and she forgot all about the glass as anger replaced all other feelings. She found Robert sitting on the couch, beer in hand, watching TV.

"Rob, why is there another girl's bra in your bathroom?"

He glanced up at her and, without flinching, replied, "That's your bra." Spring flipped. "No! This is *not* my bra! It's not even my size, you unloyal, selfish, dirty, rat!" At that point, he jumped up and pointed a finger in her face. "No, you are the selfish one. I wanted you to move in here and get a job, but you chose to go off to college, so I got fulfillment somewhere else! Oh, and loyalty? You've probably slept with every single guy on campus that let you!"

"No! I stayed pure for you because I love you and I thought you felt the same way! You—"

"Get out of here!" he cut her off. She flung the bra at him. "I will not leave! I will—" His hand came up and hit her in the face. She fell. Hatred burned in his eyes.

"I said get out, and stay out! I don't want to see your pitiful little face again." Rob shouted. Spring started to get up when he kicked her in the stomach. She fell back against the door and threw up all over the floor.

"Oh, and clean that up on your way out." He turned away and left her. She laid there with tears streaming down her face until the pain subsided enough to allow her to get back up. She stumbled her way to her car, and as she drove back to college, she vowed that she would never give her heart to another ever again.

Summer was walking lazily back to her dorm. The sweet, cool breeze that touched her face made her smile. And with her last class of the day over, she just wanted to relax before working all weekend. Out of nowhere, a massive body slammed into her, knocking her to the ground. Her books and papers flew everywhere. She laid there dazed for a second, letting out a small moan. Then she noticed that the massive body that had plowed her to the ground was wearing a John Deere baseball cap. Summer couldn't believe that the man who knocked her off her feet was also the one who flirted with her at the gas station two months ago. She tried to sit up, but only making it halfway, she grabbed her head to stop it from spinning. "You!" she shouted. Recognition flashed on his face and was soon replaced with a red blush as he awkwardly untangled himself from her.

"I am so sorry! Chad and I were tossing a football around, and I guess we got a little carried away!" He helped her to her feet and then helped her gather all of her stuff.

"I am really sorry. I—"

"It's okay. I'm fine!" She smiled to reassure him.

A red-haired guy, who she assumed was Chad, walked up and picked up the football. "Wow! Nathan, what a beautiful mess you've run into!" Chad stepped in front of Nathan and winked at her. "How about I take you out to dinner?" Nathan shot him a dirty look and in turn stepped in front of him. "No, Chad! She's mine!" He looked her way and slowly reached over and took the rest of her books.

"That is if you will have me, of course." As hard as she tried, she couldn't keep the smile from her face. "I'm not sure yet."

"Not a yes, but not a no! How about you decide while I carry your books to your dorm? We could walk together." By the time they got to her dorm building, she had agreed to eat with him Saturday night. There she left a very happy Nathan and a pouty Chad to argue about who had first dibs.

Summer smiled as she bounded up the steps with a giddy feeling high in her heart. But it faded as she walked into her room. Spring lay in bed, and her phone was ringing.

"Spree, what's wrong? I thought you were going to be at Rob's all weekend?" Without moving, Spring replied, "Nothing." The ringing had stopped as Summer walked over and picked up the phone. She noticed that Spring had several missed calls from Kent and Lori. Summer turned on the light. Spring was freshly showered and wearing sweats.

"Spree, please tell me what's going on!" Just then, the phone started ringing again, making them both jump and revealing a nasty bruise on Spring's face. Summer stood there speechless until another ring brought her out of it. She answered the phone. "Hello? Oh, hi, Dad. No! This is Summer. Ya, she's here, but I'm gonna have to call you back." She hung up the phone.

"Okay! All right! You were right, and I was wrong! He's a jerk!" Spring yelled as she threw a pillow against the wall. Summer slowly stepped closer and sat down on the bed next to Spring.

"He did this to you?" Spring couldn't answer. She just turned away as a sob unwillingly escaped. Summer wrapped her arms around her, trying to comfort her. But Spree yelped in pain and clutched her stomach. Question covered Summer's face as she slowly lifted Spring's shirt, just enough to see another angry bruise across her abdomen.

"Oh Spree, we should get this checked out by a doctor to make sure there is no major damage." she whispered as she held her. Spring shook her head no but eventually agreed to go to the hospital.

Autumn and Winter hurried into the hospital waiting room were the rest of the family waited. The sterile smell of the hospital burned in her nose. Autumn put her arms around Kent breathing in his sent to dilute the smell.

"Hey dad. Is she going to be okay?" Autumn asked. Kent smiled at her and she could see moisture in his eyes. His body was very tense and he looked angry, but his voice was calm.

"Yah, she'll be fine, just some major bruising. The police and your mom are in with her now." At that moment Lori came out of emergency with tears in her eyes. She shook her head as she spoke, "Well, even though the police have to get a report of what happened, she refuses to file charges. He beat her up, and she won't file against him. Oh, and she wants us to go home and leave her alone. She says that she just wants to go back to school." Lori started to cry.

"I just don't know what to do! I want to comfort her but she pushes me away!" Kent put his arms around her and held her.

"Well, at least she won't be seeing Rob anymore." Kent replied. Autumn stepped forward.

"Well, maybe I can talk to her." Kent nodded in approval at Autumn's suggestion.

When Autumn first saw Spring she was shocked. Half of Spring's face was swollen, black and blue. Spring gave Autumn a look that Autumn took to be annoyance.

"What do you want?" Spring grumbled. Autumn smiled and said softly, "Nothing. I just came in to see if you needed anything." Spring's face softened.

"No. I don't need anything but to get out of here and get on with my life. Oh, and for everyone to stop giving me their pity." Spring spat the last words out. Autumn nodded.

"Okay. I'll have dad get the paperwork done and I'll help you get your stuff together and drive you back to your college. Sound good?" Spring shook her head. "No! Did you not hear me? I don't want your pity."

"This isn't pity. And you know as well as I that this family won't just go home. So letting us help you a little, will help your life get back to normal." Autumn replied. Spring closed her eyes and said, "Fine. Go tell dad and let's get this over with as quickly as possible!" Autumn sighed silently with relief as she turned to go to the waiting room. *God please help us with this. And show her that she needs you.* Autumn prayed as her family came into view. They would need all the help they could get to keep this family from falling apart.

CHAPTER 6

Autumn followed Winter to their dorm building. It was a big brick building that seemed to cut into the clear blue sky. The beautiful autumn days were quickly turning into winter. All of the leaves had already fallen off, and a cold bite rode the air. When they got to the mail room, inside of their dorm building, the overseer was grinning from ear to ear, "He's already been here and gone, girl. And mmm-mm was he lookin' good!" She handed Winter a single red rose. The roses had started coming on Wednesday, and she had received one every day for a week. The overseers were no help. All they could tell them was that the man who brought it was handsome, a cowboy, and mmm-mm good. Because it was Tuesday night, they hurried to get ready and ran out to Winter's car, both a bit anxious to see who the mystery man was.

Winter already had a good idea who the mystery man was. She never showed Autumn, but each rose had a strip of paper hidden inside of the petals. Each strip had a little piece of information about the man.

> I am a bull rider. My mom and last living relative died when I was fifteen. My favorite ice cream is rocky road. My favorite color is blue. Jesus Christ is my guide and best friend. I dream of one day having a big, loving family with a little girl who can rope like a pro. My biggest fear is living the rest of my life alone.

The last note gave her an odd feeling. A yearning maybe?

When they finally got to the church, people where still parking and filing into it. This time, they were lucky enough to be able to sit together. Winter made a quick sweep over the crowd until the one man who had been on her mind all week caught her eye and started making his way over.

Autumn had sensed that something was bothering Winter, or at least consuming every inch of her brain. She had been distracted all week, would swing by the mail box two to three times a day, would be completely absent from any conversation, and now, she was acting like she was looking for someone. Although, Autumn had to admit she had been a little distracted herself. It seemed that she couldn't get Luke out of her mind. He didn't even show interest in her, so why was she attracted to him anyway?

Winter's face suddenly lit up as a big smile spread across her face. Autumn turned to see what she was smiling about.

Jacob, with a smile just as big as Winter's, was making his way toward them with a single rose in his hand.

"May I sit here?" he asked her sister as he gestured to the chair next to Winter.

"I guess you can," she replied. Was that a teasing smile Autumn saw? Winter was flirting!

"This is for you, and I dearly hope that you have received my others as well." He handed Winter the rose, his hand touching hers.

"Yes, I've received them." She reached in and pulled out a scrap of paper from the center of the rose. Autumn leaned toward her sister to read it. *I am Jacob Jackson.* He smiled. "I see you have found the hidden notes. I hoped that you would." Hidden notes! Winter hadn't told her the roses came with messages. Autumn could feel the hurt and jealousy creep into her heart. She leaned back into her own chair and tried to think about something else. To help her, she tipped her head forward so that her hair would fall to make a curtain for the sides of her face and tried to concentrate on controlling her emotions. It wasn't working. She started to pray, asking God to help her not to be mad at her sister and to help her not to succumb to jealousy.

About that time, she felt a hand brush her shoulder. Not expecting it, she jumped.

"I'm sorry. I didn't mean to startle you. I was just going to ask if I could sit here." Autumn blinked as recognition came to her face. It was Luke. But he was cleaned up this time.

"Sure! Go right ahead." Her own face had a smile now. Luke was wearing a black felt cowboy hat and a blue western shirt that made his blue eyes glow. She had a hard time concentrating on the sermon. But she wasn't the only one. Luke too was well aware of the pretty little gal sitting next to him.

After the service, Jacob asked Winter if she would allow him to take her out to dinner. "I don't know, Jacob. I still don't know—"

"Pardon me, but I have a solution to our problem. Your friend and Luke can come with us. This way, we can get to know each other better, and you won't be alone with me. It's up to you. I will wait a hundred years for you, so don't worry about me rushing you. You can take your time." Winter raised an eyebrow, but everyone could see that he was being serious. Winter let out a chuckle. "Okay, where do I need to meet you?" Autumn shook her head, which caught Winter's attention. "Oh! Autumn, you don't mind coming, do you?"

"*No*. I'll go, but you don't have to make Luke go. I don't mind being the third wheel this time." Jacob turned to Luke. "Well?" *Did he just wink at Luke?* Luke gave him a hard look and said, "I don't mind coming. I'm hungry anyway." Smiling, Jacob took Winter's hand and placed it in the crook of his elbow and led her out to her car. Autumn and Luke followed the beaming couple, and Autumn herself couldn't help but smile when she felt Luke's hand at the small of her back from time to time as they weaved their way through the crowd and out the door.

The girls followed Jacob and Luke to the restaurant, and much to the girl's surprise, when they parked, the guys came to open their doors. They had not expected that. So not knowing what to say, Autumn replied, "Oh, thank you! Wow. This place is Beautiful!" It was a cozy little restaurant designed to resemble a log cottage. It had real honeysuckle on the outside and fake grapevines inside. The lighting had a romantic glow to it that made Autumn just a little bit nervous. *This place has to be expensive.* Autumn thought to herself. Jacob and Winter got seated first, so Luke and Autumn went to find a seat across the room to give their friends some privacy. Once they sat down, Autumn spoke, "You really don't have to stay here just for Jacob's sake. I'll be fine. It's kind of a family thing." He frowned a little. "Do you want me to leave?"

"No, you're fine. I just didn't want you to think that you have to stay here in order for Jacob—"

"He didn't ask for any favors, and I was planning on asking you out anyway. He just butted in like usual." Autumn couldn't help but let a little smile out as she ran a finger over the cedar table. "You were?" He smiled back. "I'm not as romantic as Jacob. I'm not really romantic at all. I mean, I was going to send you flowers, but Jacob had already done it for your friend, and I didn't want to be a copycat. Although, I did pick these for you earlier when I was doing evening chores." He pulled a little bundle of wild flowers tied with a piece of twine out of his chest pocket.

"With your permission, I would like to get to know you better." Autumn, still smiling, took the flowers that he held out to her. "Ya, sure. That would be great. And these flowers are beautiful. Thank you! I'm surprised you found any at all this late in the season." Luke's smile grew, revealing dazzling white teeth.

"So could I pick you up on Saturday at the college for a real date?" The thought of Winter keeping secrets flashed through her mind. Autumn smiled. "I would like that! What time?" He took off his hat and set it on his knee. "Does six o'clock sound good?" Still smiling, she replied, "Yes, it does."

About that time, the waiter came by to take their orders. Just as Autumn thought, the food was pricey. Not wanting to spend a lot of money on this meal, she picked something less expencive that she knew she would like. Luke ordered quickly as well and handed the menus to the waiter. Luke started the conversation this time. "So you and Winter are related?" Autumn had to take a sip of her tea before explaining.

"Well, technically, no. We are adopted. Our parents, Kent and Lori, couldn't have kids, so they adopted."

"Oh, so your real parents gave you up?" Autumn moved her drink so the waiter could set down the basket of bread rolls.

"No, Winter's parents did because the abortion failed, but my cousins, Summer and Garrett, and I were taken away." Luke's smile had left. "I'm sorry—"

"It's okay. I don't mind talking about it. Um… would you like to pray or…"

"Sure." She was glad that he did because she was so nervous that she wasn't sure if she would have been able to do it. Autumn closed her eyes and listened to the roughness of Luke's voice as he prayed. He prayed like someone who had made a habit of doing so. After the prayer, Autumn reached out to grab a bread roll, bumping into his when their hands reached for the same one.

"Sorry!" they both said at the same time. Letting go of the roll, they both grabbed another and proceeded to eat.

"So did you ever get in touch with your parents?" Luke questioned. Autumn smiled. She was used to people being curious about her past.

"Yes, I am actually staying with my biological dad every other weekend until he leaves to take a job out west." At that time, the waiter came by with their food. Luke immediately cut into his steak and dipped it into his potatoes.

"He lives in Glennville?"

Autumn almost giggled. "Oh no, he lives near Miles City. He likes it there. I don't see how. I personally long to be back in the sweet country grasses of Hickory. I guess that's part of the reason I like the Cowboy Church so much. It's in the country."

Luke raised an eyebrow. "Hickory?" Autumn couldn't help but let out a giggle this time. "Yes, it is a real town! It may be small, but it's real!" It was Luke's turn to laugh, and the way it rumbled through his chest made her heart race.

"Oh, I know! It's just that I came from that area as well. My family lives in Silow." Autumn almost choked on her chicken al freado. "Are you serious? You went to school at Silow?" Autumn asked.

"Well, no. I was homeschooled." Luke explained. Autumn took another bite of food.

"So what about your family?" Luke took a sip of his lemonade before answering. "I have one brother, older, and one sister, younger. She's a senior in high school. Our mother didn't homeschool her. My dad is a doctor, and my mom takes care of a small herd of sheep." Autumn, still curious, asked another question. "What made you move all the way out here?" Luke's expression turned thoughtful. "I had to get away. My parents are the controlling type. I had watched my mother try desperately to hook my brother up with girls that she wanted, and when he chose a girl that she didn't approve of, she was not happy. Ellie is a good woman. She just didn't come from a more successful family. Anyway, my parents tried to change them and hounded them. The almost constant family fights and not enough space caused

Sam and Ellie to split for a while. But they are still trying to make it work. Sam got a job in town, and they don't visit very often. Mom made being at home miserable, trying to hook me up with girls and constantly complaining about…" He waved a hand in the air, not being able to come up with an example. "Something. So when I read in the paper about a job working as a farm hand, I left." Luke smiled, still reminiscing. "Started working for this crazy eighty-year-old man who said he would rather die being trampled by cows than retire. Having no family, he had to hire people. Learned everything I know about farming from him. He took a stupid eighteen-year-old and passed down a whole lot of wisdom. Last year, the crazy old goat up and died on me, left me his whole farm. It had to have been God 'cause stuff like that just don't happen anymore." Luke, realizing that he had been rambling, blushed and asked, "So what about your real mom?" Autumn smiled. "She died in a car crash along with my aunt and uncle, Summer and Garrett's parents. Anyway, my dad was our last living relative, and I guess he went crazy because they say he locked us in a closet and left two, two-year-olds and a one-year-old to die." She smiled to lighten the mood. "But he got saved in prison and is now trying to live his life for God."

Luke had stopped eating by this point. "I'm sorry I brought it up. So are there just the four of you?" Autumn smiled again, "Its okay. Like I said, I don't mind talking about it. And there are actually five of us, Winter, me,

Seasons of Life

Summer, Spring, and Garrett. All the same age except Garrett. He's younger. And yes, we are named after seasons. Kent and Lori has a sense of humor!" Autumn and Luke laughed with each other. After they quit laughing, they fell into silence. Luke looked at her for a while before asking, "So what was your old name?" She smiled and just simply said, "Candice." He had gotten lost in her dark, green, hypnotizing eyes.

"Wow. They are both such pretty names. I'm not sure which one to call you." Still smiling, she replied, "Whichever you like. When they adopted my cousins and I, they just turned our first names into middle names and left our last names alone. So we still have our real parents last names." Luke nodded, and they both took another bite of food.

"Hey, Luke I have a question. What's with Jacob? Why does he talk like that?"

Winter had gotten up to go to the bathroom and smiled at the way Autumn and Luke had been so deep into conversation that they didn't notice her walk right by them. They probably didn't even notice that they were leaning toward each other. On her way out, she was about to round the corner that lead to the dining room when she heard Autumn say, "What's with Jacob? Why does he talk like that?" Because Autumn and Luke's booth was on the other side of the wall that divided the dining area from the bathroom entrances, she could hear their conversation clearly. She flattened herself to the wall and focused on listening. She heard Luke clear his throat.

"Well, as I understand it, his mother loved Shakespeare and any book or movie that had the old language. He was really close to his mom. As far as I know, I am the only one he talks normal to, and even then, it's only when he's upset or sick. I think he does it out of remembrance and also to protect himself from hurt. I think he figured that if people had to make fun of him, then he would give them a reason." Winter frowned in concentration.

"Its most likely going to get him hurt because Winter will see him more as a charmer instead of being serious. Does he do this with all his interest?" Autumn asked. There was a long pause. Luke's gaze was intense.

"I have known Jacob since we were four. Winter has been his only interest. He hasn't had any others."

Winter's head spun, and the guilt from eavesdropping was getting to her. So she hurriedly went back to her table. Jacob was smiling at her approach.

"My beauty returns!" Before he could say anything else, she jumped in, not being able to resist the urge to hear his side of the story, "Jacob, why do you talk like that?" His face froze, and his smile slowly fell as his gaze drifted downward. He let out a sigh, and a soft smile of remembrance appeared. He fumbled with his napkin.

"My mom… she…" he glanced around as he shifted his weight. He opened his mouth again to answer but closed it and rubbed his face with his hands.

"I… can we talk about this somewhere else?" He looked at her with a begging plead. She stared into his violet-colored eyes, and she could see the hurt. She nodded. "Sure. Okay," she whispered. They stared at each other's serious face for a while before he slowly rose and walked around the table, took her hand, and helped her up. Being this close to him made her feel small. Even though he was smaller than Luke, his still looked huge to Winter when she was close enough to see faint lines of muscles under his shirt. Sensing her discomfort, he stepped back and went to pay. So Winter, catching her breath again, gathered her stuff and went to inform Autumn.

"Hey, Autumn, I'm going with Jacob. I'll see ya later." She turned and left before her sister could say anything. Concerned, Autumn started to get up to go after her, but Luke stopped her.

"Luke?"

He pulled her back to the table. "Just trust me. Its best to just leave them be." He had seen that look on Jacob's face before and knew what was going on.

In silence, Jacob drove her to his house that he had bought from Luke, where he led her to the swing that attached to the porch. After she sat down, he sat across from her on the porch railing. He took off his hat and leaned back against the post. The moonlight illuminated his face, and the cool breeze tossed his black hair.

"My mother was all that I had. She wanted to teach me how to be a gentleman, like in the old movies. She wanted me to be the opposite of my father. The fancy speech was only a game, but when she died, I guess I never stopped. Since then, only you and Luke have heard me talk normal." There was silence. He turned to look at her. "I… I really like you, so if… if you don't like it when I talk like that, then I think I can try to stop—"

"How can you care for someone you barely know?" Winter asked.

Jacob chuckled. "I uh… I asked God that, and he hasn't answered me yet on that one. I know it sounds stupid." He shook his head and looked out into the yard. Winter stood up and took his hand in hers. "I don't mind the way you talk. In fact, I kind of like it." He turned to find her smiling. He slid off the railing as she intertwined their fingers. "Maybe if we both pray, he will answer that question for us one day." Suggested Winter as she smiled up at him.

Jacob smiled at her reply. "Ya, maybe he will."

Winter led him to the truck. "You had better get me back to the school, or Autumn may get worried."

Seasons of Life

"Whatever you wish, my dear. May I get the door for you?" Winter laughed as he opened the door and helped her in.

CHAPTER 7

Spring hurried down to the main lobby. It had a big screen TV where most of the football fans who couldn't get home to watch it congregated. After what happened with Robert, she couldn't stand going home to Kent and Lori. She had visited them a couple times, but their nagging and prodding about going to church and them trying to hook her up with guys they liked drove her crazy. The men they liked weren't any better. All men were the same, all after the same thing. If she wanted to be with someone it would have to be her choice. So she didn't go home unless she absolutely had to.

Spring bounded into the crowded football frenzy, snagged a handful of popcorn, high stepped over several people, and wiggled into the last remaining space on the couch. Everyone scrunched together to make room, but she still ended up halfway sitting on her neighbors lap. He turned toward her. "Well, you're not shy, are you?" Without even glancing at him, she replied, "No, not really. Who's in the lead?" He smiled. "The Broncs. My names Keith, but you can call me whatever you want to." Spring turned to look at him this time. She studied him closely as she slowly put another piece of popcorn into her mouth. "Okay, Keith, my name is Spree." He put his arm around her. "So does this mean we can be friends?" She looked at his arm and then raised an eyebrow. His face turned serious. "There is more room this way." She narrowed her eyes. "What kind of friends?" He didn't miss a beat. "Any kind you would like." Spring burst into laughter, and they continued to flirt until Summer walked in and beckoned Spring to follow her.

Spring got off Keith's lap and smiled as he hollered, "Come back soon!" She walked up to Summer. "What's up?"

"Spree, who's the guy?" Spring glanced over her shoulder. "Oh, that's Keith. He's a friend."

"Just a friend? Come on, Spree! Don't insult me. I am not stupid. You two were practically all over each other. So is this number three since Robert? When are you going to stop?"

Spring crossed her arms in front of her chest. "I will do whatever I want to, and besides, being with someone makes me happy." Summer frowned. "Then why did you dump the last one? He wanted a long-term relationship." Spring rolled her eyes. "I didn't want to get that serious. He was talking like we were going to get married next week. Besides, I just want to have fun and be happy." Summer wanted to scream at her. "Oh! So having sex with the guy isn't serious. Thanks for clearing that up! This is not making you happy, Spree! Why can't you see that you are making yourself miserable?"

Spring narrowed her eyes as the anger inside of her boiled. She pointed a finger in Summer's face. "Wrong. And stay out of my life." She spun around and sat back down on Keith's lap even though there was now room on the couch. Keith smiled at Summer. "Don't be jealous, baby!" Then he winked at her.

"You wish," Summer replied before she turned to go up to her dorm.

Spring, still fuming, turned toward Keith and wrapped her arms around him.

"Hey, Keith, is your car accessible?" Keith smiled and nodded.

"Good. I'm bored. Let's get out of here." She led the way out, not noticing the wink Keith gave to another guy in the room.

Summer shook her head as she watched Spring leave with Keith. Why couldn't Spring see that she was ruining her life? Unless Spree was flirting with a guy, she just sat and moped. Sure, she did well in school, but school had always been easy for her. She sighed and turned from the window to get a change of clothes and shower. Working at the nearby dairy barn left her quite smelly.

Seasons of Life

Just as she was heading to the bathroom, her phone rang. It was Nathan. Smiling, sour mood already lifting, she answered, "Hey, you off work already?" She asked. He chuckled. "Yeah, I hurried as fast as I could. You know, next semester, we need to work out our schedules better 'cause seeing your beautiful face only every other Saturday sucks!" She laughed. "Yes, it does! So what are we going to do tonight?"

"Oh, that's a surprise! I can't tell you!"

She smiled at his playful flirting. "Nate, you know I hate surprises!" He chuckled and then, in a seductive voice, replied, "Then why is my beautiful, cow-poop-covered angel smiling?" There was silence as she turned and looked out the window. There he was, smiling back at her, waving.

"Nate! What are—"

"Ah-ah. No questions. Just hurry with the shower. It's cold out here!" She laughed as she hung up the phone and hurried off to the bathroom.

CHAPTER 8

Autumn filled her bowl with poorly made stew. Her father didn't cook very well, and the food that he had there was usually junk food. But he insisted that he cook for her. They ate in the living room like always so he could watch the NASCAR race. She didn't see her father much this semester, but it was mutual. He was extremely busy with moving and getting ready for his new job, and she spent as much time as she could with Luke. In fact, this was going to be the last time she was going to be able to see her dad for at least three years.

He broke her train of thought. "So that boy is coming when?"

"Fra—Dad, he's not a boy. He's twenty-five, and he'll be here in about fifteen minutes." Luke had gone on the rodeo circuit last year to clear his head and just for the fun of it. So naturally, he made friends; in fact, his old roping partner begged him to rope with him today when his new partner got injured. So Autumn was going along to watch.

"So, Dad, are you sure you don't want me to stay and help you pack?" He smiled and shook his head. "No. You go ahead to that cow thing. Besides, they hired a moving company to move me and my stuff. I've got to be out of here by tomorrow, so the moving people are coming at five." She nodded. "Do you want me to at least help you pack up what's left?" Again he shook his head no.

"The bowls go into the trash. The TV and the chairs can't be packed, and the remaining stew will go with me."

They sat and watched the race for a while, but Autumn's mind was elsewhere. She still hadn't asked her dad about the past. She sighed. It was now or wait three years, and she certainly didn't want to ask him over the phone. She looked over at her dad. Noticing her change of mood, he cocked his head a little, and his face had a questioning look to it.

"What's wrong, Candy?" Candy was a childhood nickname he had given her. Even though her name was changed, he still called her by it, and she didn't mind. She took a breath and prayed it wouldn't ruin everything. "Why did you give up? When… when Mom died. Why did you leave us to die?" He froze, completely off guard. When at last what she had said sunk in, he let out a sigh.

"When you mom, aunt, and uncle died in that wreck, I… I lost it, I guess. I mean I was you and your cousin's last relative, and I missed your mom so much. I felt so alone."

He chuckled. "She wanted to go to the mall with your aunt, and James, your uncle, said that he was going to be the man in the family and go with them. They picked on me pretty bad. But I didn't want to go, so they left you guys with me. That was no problem 'cause I loved you all so much! But when I heard, I just wanted to forget. So I cleaned out the closet and put you in there so you would be safe, and I left to get drunk. I guess I got too drunk and ended up halfway across the US." He paused and looked at her.

"I am so sorry! I had meant to come back and care for you all, but I messed up, and by the time I came to my senses, the neighbor had found you and the police had found me." There was silence. Autumn didn't know what to say. She had spent half her childhood wondering what she had done that was so bad that her own daddy didn't want her. But after she accepted Christ as her savior, she had learned to forgive and realized that it wasn't her fault. But now, part of her wanted to yell at him and tell him how it made her feel to know that her real father abandoned her. Her heart hurt and tears pushed at the back of her eyes. She didn't want to believe him. She ducked her head to hide her face from him. *Oh God! Please help me do what is right for this situation.* Autumn silently prayed. "I hope you will forgive me." Her dad said. The sadness was evident on his face. And she could tell that, what he had done to her and her cousions, had haunted him everyday. As a tear fell down her cheek, she forced a smile and replied, "I forgave you a long time ago. I just needed to hear your side of the story. And I love you just as much now as I did then." Tears were now rolling down his face as he cried openly in front of her.

"I am so sorry. You have no idea how sorry I am! I should have been there for you." She shushed him and replied, "But you're in my life now." Tears rolled down her own face as she set her stew down and hugged him.

Luke rumbled his old truck down the potholed road that lead to the house of Autumn's real father. The hair on the back of his neck bristled. He noticed the look of suspicion on the faces of the people he drove by and the peering eyes that peaked through covered windows. He pulled into the drive of the run-down house that Autumn was supposed to be in. Keys in his hand, he walked to the door all the while feeling eyes watching his every move. He knocked on the door and a frown crossed his face when he noticed scratches on the bars that protected the windows. He reached out and touched the deep groves across the bars. But soon, his thoughts of people trying to get into the house were interrupted by the sound of bolts and locks sliding on the door. Before he knew it, the most beautiful face smiled up at him. A smile of his own spread across his face.

"Are you ready?" He asked. Her green eyes sparkled like emeralds.

"Yeah." She spun around and gave her dad, who now stood by her at the door, a light hug and grabbed her overnight bag.

"Thanks for offering to drive me back to the college! Winter had an unexpected date so she took the car." Autumn stated. The silkiness of her raven black hair caught him off guard. Recovering, he replied, "Not a problem!" Turning to her dad he held out his hand.

"You must be Frank. I'm Luke Buckner." To his surprise her father smiled.

"Nice to meet you. Now you two get on out of here and have fun!" He turned to Autumn. "I'll call you when I get settled in. In fact I'll call you often." He hung his head for a second before he met her gaze.

"I'm going to miss you. Miss you a lot." Frank whispered. Autumn nodded, "Yeah, I'm going to miss you too. Thanks for talking with me. It ment a lot to me." Autumn said and gave him another hug before turning to leave. Luke took her by the hand and carried her bag to the truck. After opening the door for her, he put her bag in the truck bed and drove off. Autumn's hand tingled from his touch. That was the first time he had held her hand. But even in this bliss, she noticed something was wrong.

"Are you okay?" She asked. He gave her a faint smile.

"Kind of a rough part of town he lives in, don't ya think?" He questioned. She smiled, her gorgeous emerald-green eyes looking back at him, framed by her soft black hair. He had an overwhelming urge to run his fingers through it.

"He won't be living there long. In fact, tonight he's leaving out west to start his new union job." Relief was obvious on his face, and when he pulled over to get gas, he wrapped his arms around her without thinking. She hugged him back, happiness bubbling inside of her. She breathed in his scent. It reminded her of hay and cool country breezes, and she melted into his firm embrace. Without realizing it, she nuzzled her head into his chest and sighed. Her movement, mistook by Luke, made him release her.

"I'm sorry. I shouldn't have done that."

A confused look crossed her face. "Don't be." Luke smiled lightly and started to climb out to fill up his truck. Happiness filled him at the thought of her allowing him to hug her, but had he gone too far? His thoughts were interrupted.

"So we are going to the rodeo, but where is your horse?" Autumn was leaning out the window, waiting for his reply.

Luke burst into laughter, immediately lightening the mood. "At the rodeo grounds with Paul and Jacob! Wait until you see us doing what we love best!" A smile equal to his own told him that she indeed couldn't wait.

Frank watched his daughter climb into Luke's truck and drive away. Heavy guilt and sadness washed over him. He wasn't surprised to feel doubt about leaving for this job, but it was something God had wanted him to do. He hated his past, and he knew that he couldn't change it, or even make up for it, but he could at least let her know that he loved her. He was glad that she had given him permission to be part of her life again. It was a start anyway. Sighing, he went inside to finish packing. But instead, he sat down at the table and prayed for the safety of his daughter and that young man.

Luke and Autumn pulled up to the roping arena and backed up to his horse trailer. When they walked up to the horses, some of the other cowboys converged around them. Most just slapped Luke on the back and said, "Hey! Luke, nice to see you're back!" And some of the men would walk up to him and say, "Hey, Luke, where did you come across the pretty, black-haired filly?" Luke would just smile, shake his head, and say, "It's nice to see you too." Eventually, Autumn realized (after noticing that Luke did not, in fact, bring a black horse) that they were talking about her, making her blush. By the time they got to his horse to get ready, she had gathered that most of the men competing thought a lot of Luke and were truly glad to see him.

The smile on Luke's face as he checked his saddle and practiced with the rope told Autumn that he kind of missed the rodeo. He noticed her watching him, and he smiled at her. "Do you miss the rodeo, Luke?" Still smiling, he replied, "A little, but joining the rodeo takes money and time. I would be abandoning the farm if I rodeoed full time. In fact, I'm still trying to catch up from the one year I did rodeo."

Autumn tipped her head to the side a little. "But didn't you make money at it?"

Luke chuckled. "I am good, but there are a lot of others who are better. I broke about even. Now I just do rodeos that are close by for the fun of it, or to help out a friend, like today. Oh, speaking of Paul." Luke waved to catch Paul's attention. Autumn turned to see who Paul was. The tall native American sauntered over and embraced his friend. His long black hair was pulled back into a ponytail, and his dark eyes sparkled with laughter.

Paul, who was just as tall as Luke, had started to inquire of Autumn when one of the bull riders shouted, "Hey! Who let the Indian in here?" Autumn, shocked by the comment, relaxed a little when Paul winked at her and smiled at the bull rider and said, "This Indian can outdo ya any day of the week!" The two laughed, along with a few other cowboys who had overheard the conversation. Autumn shook her head as the playful banter continued. Luke laughed at his friend. "Hey, Paul, this is Autumn Leaves." This was the second time Luke had taken her hand in his. It sent shivers through her. Paul took off his hat and shook her hand. "Nice to meet ya." Luke stepped forward. "Autumn, of course, this is Paul, and as you can tell, he is Indian. Well, half Indian actually. His mother was a full blood." Paul smiled at Luke. "Now, Luke, she doesn't care to know my history." Paul slapped Luke on the arm. "Come on. Its about to start." Luke took Autumn by the hand again to show her where to sit, and then he went to get ready.

While she was walking over to the bleachers, she spotted Winter with Jacob. As she got closer toward them, she heard Jacob say, "How about a kiss for good luck?" Winter smiled and flung herself into his arms and kissed him. About that time, Paul shouted, "Hey, Romeo! Are you gonna ride or just kiss your girl?" Jacob let Winter go, and with a wink and a smile, he shouted back, "I shall do both. Thank you! Not that it's any of your business." Autumn jabbed Winter in the ribs and raised an eyebrow.

"I didn't know you were going to be here." Autumn stated.

Startled, Winter placed her hand over her heart to try to slow down her pulse. "You shouldn't scare me like that! And also, you should know that I go wherever Jacob goes." Autumn gave a knowing nod and both girls went to sit down.

The rodeo started with the kids. They watched as kids of all ages rode sheep and calves down the arena. They reminded Autumn of little rag dolls tied to the end of a dog's tail, being jerked this way and that. Out of the arena came several of the kids looking like dust monsters with grins so big that Autumn couldn't help but smile at the next generation of "rodeoers." When the bull riding started, the girls cheered for Jacob. The look of complete seriousness on Jacob's face as he rode the full eight seconds had Winter mesmerized. After the buzzer sounded, he leaped off the bull and barely landed on his feet before he took off running for the fence. He stumbled once but regained balance and finally made it. Once out of harm's way, he took a bow at the cheering audience and blew a kiss in Winter's direction. At that point, Winter stood up and told Autumn that she was going to congratulate Jacob.

Eventually, after the barrel racing and a few other events, the team roping started. When Luke and Paul's turn came, Autumn couldn't help but notice the pure concentration on Luke's face and how he instinctively backed his horse into the roper's box, lariat in his teeth. He removed it from his mouth, checking it, then glanced at Paul who gave him a nod in return. Autumn caught a smile that had danced briefly across Luke's face as he turned his head to face the arena. Then with Luke's nod, the calf shoot snapped open, and the thunder of hooves sounded. With a quick toss from both men, the calf was stretched out between them. Smiles covered both of the men's faces with the announcement that they had the leading time.

Autumn went to congratulate Luke as Winter had done for Jacob earlier. In fact, she didn't even know where Winter was at the moment. But all thoughts of her sister vanished once she spotted Luke. Out of instinct, she wrapped her arms around him in a big hug.

"I'm so happy for you!" Luke's heartbeat quickened, and he hugged her back.

"Well, maybe I should take you to rodeos more often! Do I get hugs if I miss the calf completely as well?" Autumn giggled at Luke's remark.

"Yeah, no kidding! Do I get a hug too?" Autumn turned to face Paul just as Luke was giving him a stern look and replied, "No! Go find your own hug." Luke replied. Paul laughed. "Yeah, I wish I could. But unlike you, I don't have time for women."

Luke shook his head and gave Paul a small smile. "You'll figure it out sooner or later. Keep in touch." They slapped each other on the back as they both went to pack up. As Luke started to unsaddle his horse, thoughts of Paul crossed his mind. Paul had once told him that he was lonely, but he didn't want to take the time to find the right one. So after a few years of bad relationships, he just kind of wrote all women as being the same—pure evil, painted over to attract men in a plot to ruin them. But today, Paul's resolve seemed to crumble a little. Luke remembered how Paul had looked at Autumn as she went to sit down. Luke had asked him what he was looking at, and without hesitation, Paul replied, "Your girlfriend. She's pretty." Paul was the straightforward type, and Luke knew that, but he still couldn't hide the jealousy that he had felt. Taking on a joking tone to cover up how he felt, he replied, "Yes, she is pretty, but you can find another pretty girl to ogle at." Paul let out a laugh and softly said, "But none as pretty as that." Luke turned so Paul couldn't see his face. "Hey, come on. Let's go warm up the horses." Luke sighed as he came back to reality. Paul was his good friend. He shouldn't have gotten cranky with him.

At this point, Autumn interrupted his thoughts. "Hey, Luke, where do you want me to put this?" He turned to face her. Her beautiful green eyes peered up at him. And she looked so cute standing there in *his* horse trailer, holding *his* saddle blanket. He stepped forward to take it from her, but getting distracted, he ran his fingers through her hair before he lightly placed a kiss on her soft-looking lips. He stepped back and took the saddle blanket.

"Sorry. I…" He shook his head and turned to put the blanket up, inwardly scolding himself and, without realizing it, mumbling softly out loud too. But when he turned back to her, she wrapped her arms around his neck and kissed him back. When she pulled back, she snuggled up to him in a hug.

"I figured you needed that, considering you seem to have a lot on your mind."

He smiled. "Thanks." They stood there for a few seconds, holding each other before they pulled apart. Not knowing what to say, he smiled and laced his fingers in with hers and led her out of the trailer.

They finished packing in silence until Autumn spoke up. "Luke, where's Winter and Jacob?" Luke looked around and couldn't find Jacob's trailer.

"I don't know. They must have left already." But Autumn couldn't help but worry about Winter. Winter had been spending a lot of time with Jacob lately. Even more time than Autumn had spent with Luke. Autumn had also noticed that Winter's grades were slipping a little. When Autumn mentioned it to her she just laughed and remarked about how she was still passing her classes, that she should forget about it, and to quit worrying. Then the other day she was over at Luke's place for the first time, Luke was showing her around the ranch when they came up on Winter and Jacob leaning against a tree kissing. Jacob and Luke made short conversation, but Winter refused to meet her gaze. Winter refused to talk about it as well. Autumn let out a sigh, she knew that she shouldn't dwell so much on things that she couldn't control. So she said a quick prayer for her sister and left her worries with God. Feeling better, she helped Luke finish packing up his gear and then followed him back to the audience stands. They watched the rest of the rodeo before leaving. As they walked to his truck, Luke asked, "Hey, do you mind coming with me to my house and help me unload the horses before I take you back to the college?" Autumn smiled. "Sure, I don't mind." Luke helped her into the truck.

"If you're hungry, I make a good steak." Luke added. Autumn laughed, and it sounded like music to Luke's ears. Autumn smiled over at him. "I can't wait! I'm half starved!" Luke took her hand in his and laughed as he turned the truck toward the exit gate.

CHAPTER 9

Spring slammed her car door and proceeded to walk to her dorm. Her head hurt from trying to hold back tears of anger. She felt filthy in her strapless black dress. It was still crumpled from being with her boyfriend, well, ex-boyfriend. Anger ignited inside of her chest once more at the memory of him dumping her and telling her to leave. *How could he say that when earlier that night, he claimed his love for me? Besides, wasn't I supposed to be the one who would dump him? I was planning on doing it soon anyway. But instead, he used me one last time before sending me on my way!*

She caught her reflection in a window she was passing. She was defiantly pretty. Her long legs looked elegant, peeking out of the knee-length dress, and her slender arms were accented perfectly by golden hair that lay across her shoulders. But even with seeing herself, she felt like trash. *But isn't this what I wanted? Just a loose, fun, not-serious relationship? Then how come I felt so horrible, almost dead, inside?* The excitement of a new relationship got duller and duller with each new guy that came into her life. She shoved the thoughts from her mind. *All well,* she thought as she willed her heart to harden just a little bit more. *This way, I can start over. Everyone back home thinks I'm loose and rude. Well, why not just embrace my fate. I'll find someone new, then another, and I'll make myself happy.*

She was reaching for the door of her dorm building when she heard someone running up behind her. It was one of Keith's friends.

"Spree, I just heard what Keith did to you! I am so sorry. If it matters much, I punched him for you." Spring stared at him long and hard. Erik and Keith were close. It would put a dent in Keith's ego to have Spring bounce back so quickly. If it was with his best friend, it would be even better. In fact, she could claim that she and Erik had something all along anyway. She and Erik do flirt every once in a while.

"Are you angry with him, Erik?" she asked in a cool kind of voice. Not hearing what he was expecting startled him. "I… uh… well, yeah! I would have never done something like that, and I can't believe he would either." Spring smiled and leaned against the wall, making sure that her leg showed as much as possible through the split in her dress.

"Well, I have to admit that I was shocked when he dumped me, but I was kind of relieved too. 'Cause I like you, Erik. I have for a while. I didn't want to get in between you and Keith, but I noticed that I was flirting with you more and more, so I was going to leave him anyway." She turned her head and let her hair fall over her face, pretending to be ashamed or embarrassed. It worked. Erik walked up to her and wrapped his arms around her. "You really liked me?" He turned her face to look into his. The innocent look she placed on her face hooked him. She kissed him to seal the deal. He started to go back for another kiss, but she shoved him back.

"I'll see you tomorrow then?"

His confused look changed to a smile. "Yes, I'll see you tomorrow."

Spring turned and sauntered up to the door, making sure to turn to look at him before she shut the door behind her. When she was sure that he couldn't see her anymore, she let the act fall and started to climb the stairs to her dorm, glad that her sister left for the weekend. But unfortunately, what Spring did not see was Erik climbing into Keith's car and giving him a high five.

CHAPTER 10

Luke pulled into the college parking lot to pick Autumn up for Christmas break. She was beautiful. With snow falling on her soft black, raven hair and her green eyes smiling at him, he found it hard to breath. "Hey" was all he could manage to get out. She smiled back at him as he took her bag and helped her into the truck. Luke cleared his throat. "I'm sorry about the heater. It quit working the other day. Are you cold?" Autumn shivered. "A little." Luke handed her a blanket, and she wrapped it around herself. But after a while, it became apparent that she was still cold as she started to shiver nonstop. Luke hesitated as nervousness coursed through him, but took a deep breath and said it any way, "Maybe you should sit over here, next to me." She looked at him for a moment before moving on over beside him. Luke put his arm around her to help warm her up, and it made his heart race. She felt so tiny at his side, delicate almost. And her smell was intoxicating. He had to get his mind on something else, start a conversation at least, or being this close to her would get the better of him. Luke took a deep breath. "So what's your favorite thing about Christmas with your folks?" She smiled, "Well… um." Luke couldn't help but notice that she sounded a little bit nervous herself. *Well, at least I'm not the only one.* He thought to himself. Autumn continued to talk.

"I guess my favorite thing would be seeing everyone and doing stuff together. Like, drinking hot chocolate, sleeping under Christmas lights, oh! And hearing dad tell the Christmas story! You see he likes to act it out so it can be quite funny. One year we had some relatives over and our Aunt Tilly had just had baby boy. So dad used him for baby Jesus. The poor kid cried all the way through the story!" Luke glanced at her briefly. Seeing the happiness on her face as she reminisced, he silently welcomed the long drive home.

Luke took Autumn home instead of taking her to meet his family. He wasn't really sure himself that he wanted to introduce her. Just thinking about it filled him with dread, and he could feel the stress creeping back. But he soon forgot about his family when he met hers. They were nice, and everyone was friendly. Although he could tell that they had their own problems as well, he gladly accepted their invite to stay for supper. Winter and Jacob hadn't arrived yet, so when they did finally show up, the whole greeting scene started all over.

Kent stood up to shake Jacob's hand. "Hey, glad that you made it! You must be Jacob Jackson. Nice to meet you!" Jacob bowed. "Pleasure is mine." Kent just smiled, unsure what to say. Even though Winter had told everyone how he talked and why, Kent still wasn't ready for it. But it didn't faze Lori any. She was all smiles. "This is great, girls! We can finally use the other end of this enormous table your dad bought." This helped bring Kent back around. He walked up to his wife and wrapped his arms around her.

"But, honey, I thought you loved this table?" A teasing spark in his gray-blue eyes let everyone know he was just picking a joke. He kissed her, but when it started to last a little long, she pushed him back and slapped his chest.

"Now don't get fresh in front of the kids. Save that for later." Lori turned to go into the kitchen, making sure to flip her blond hair. Kent whispered, "Hey. Hey, Lori, is that a hint? I can't remember what our code word is." The room erupted into laughter, and "gross!" or "Now I'll have nightmares!" echoed across the room.

After the laughter died down and prayer was said, everyone settled down to fill their plates. Lori smiled, happiness bubbling inside of her. "Now all we need is Summer and Spring to bring someone!" Summer smiled and reminded her mother why she hadn't, and Spring just rolled her eyes.

"I just didn't think to… I mean, I know we are dating, but it's not that serious. We just hang out together when we can." Autumn leaned in to the table toward Summer. "And how often is that?" Summer smiled and shook her head. "Not that often. Our schedules are horrible to work with! I'm serious. If I'm not working, he is. So we mostly just text." Summer took a sip of sweet tea. "To be honest, I feel like we are more like good friends than a couple." She grabbed a roll from the basket that was being passed around and then turned to Spring.

"So Spree, how is your new boyfriend?"

Spring frowned at her. "What is there to say? He's fine. Anyway, enough about me. Hey, Garrett, so how are you doing in the dating world?" Garrett broke the silence in the room and replied, "Well, Spree, I have decided that I am going to let God pick my wife, and so far, I haven't found her yet."

Spring snorted, "How exactly does that work? Does God shout down, 'Thou shall not talk to her'?" She chuckled to herself.

"Oh, that's funny!" She said. Garrett just smiled at her. "Well, sis, not exactly. If I meet a girl I like, then I pray about her, and in God's time, I get a yes or no answer. And no, I don't hear a booming voice from heaven. Usually, just subtle signs. So far, I've only got no answers. But until I get a yes, I'll wait to date."

Kent smiled at his son. "That's great, son! I'm proud! Letting God pick you future spouse is a wise decision."

Seasons of Life

Everyone in the room agreed, except Spring who slid farther down in her chair, feeling even more out of place in her own home.

They talked and ate. Almost everyone enjoyed themselves. After dinner, the evening began to wind down, and Luke decided that he couldn't put off going to see his family any longer. Standing up, he addressed Jacob, "Well, we had better get going. My parents don't know we are coming, and they will be in bed soon." With a sigh, Jacob stood up. "If we must." He replied, sending Winter a wink. "Well, good-night. It was nice to meet you," Luke said as he shook Kent and Lori's hands. Jacob followed Luke's example, and they both tipped their hats to Summer and Spring, then sent a wave to Garrett, who had been unusually silent the whole evening. The two couples finally made it to the door. Autumn followed Luke to his truck 'cause she didn't want to say good-bye to him at the door where Winter and Jacob stood.

"So are you coming over tomorrow?" Autumn asked. Luke smiled. "Well, with it being Christmas, I figured your family would like to be alone. I know that's how mine is. But if it's all the same to you, I'll come over the day after."

"Okay." She said as she nodded.

Luke thought she might have looked a little disappointed. He stood there, taking his time looking at her, remembering her smell and how she had felt in his arms. Nervousness coursed through him as he reached out and took her hand. "Hey, Autumn, how would your dad feel about me kissing you right now?" She smiled, and he thought he saw a blush. "He probably wouldn't care as long as you didn't get fresh." He looked into her eyes and slowly pulled her over to him, giving her plenty of time to pull away if she wanted to. But she didn't. She slid over to him and fell perfectly into his embrace, and she buried her face into his chest. He brushed his hand across her cheek, moving her silky, black hair behind her ear. Then he tilted her face up to his and gently kissed her. Her lips felt so soft. He pulled away, not wanting to go too far. He looked into her eyes as he stroked her face one last time before he left.

"I'll see you later," he whispered. She gave him another quick kiss before leaving his arms to head to the house.

Autumn turned around to see Winter and Jacob *still* kissing, kissing a little too deep. Autumn had just said Winter's name to get them to back off a little when the door came open and their father's skinny frame shadowed the doorframe.

"Winter, I think you have said good-bye long enough," Kent's stern voice made the couple jump. Luke shook his head. "Sir, I am sorry for my friend's behavior. He is not normally like this." Kent, puzzled about why Luke would apologize, said, "Don't be. I'm just doing my job, and besides, why are you the one apologizing?" Luke nodded and gave Autumn's hand a little squeeze before he let it go and hopped in his truck. Autumn continued to walk into the house, squeezing past Winter and Jacob after noticing for the first time the faces of her family in the living room window, each seemingly with a different expression. Summer looked amused. Spring looked like she was deep in thought, and Garrett looked disgusted. Jacob, who had been staring at the ground, glanced up and gave Winter an apologetically look, softly kissed her hand, and left without saying a word. His face burned with embarrassment. He had gone too far, and he knew it, and the sad thing was he couldn't bring himself to ask Kent's forgiveness. Kent had rules as a father, and Jacob had caused Winter to break them. As he climbed into his truck, he could hear Winter argue with her father. Rubbing a hand over his face, he said a quick prayer for courage so he would be able to apologize tomorrow. And he drove away.

Autumn kicked off her shoes after Luke and Jacob left and tried to ignore her family's teasing as well as her father's discussion with Winter about proper dating etiquette. Winter should have known better.

"I am an adult, Dad! I have the right to make my own decisions. And before you ask, no, we have not had sex, and I plan on keeping it that way! But I still have the right to decide how far is too far!" Winter shouted. Kent gave her a stern look. "Winter, you know the rules of this house. Yes, I know you are an adult, but when you are on my property, you follow my guidelines! And besides, they are set in place to keep you from being tempted to go too far."

Winter rolled her eyes. "It was just a kiss!!!" Garrett snorted, "Sis, it looked like you were eating each other's face off." Kent held a hand up to Garrett. "It is not your time to speak Garret." Winter, almost in tears, shouted, "You all are horrible! Can't a girl have a little privacy!" Kent looked at his daughter and said softly, "Winter, I think you need less privacy." Winter frowned and fled to her room, passing a zombie-like Spring on the way.

After a while, Autumn said good-night to Kent and Lori and headed upstairs herself. Her mind was a torrent of emotions. She felt elated from kissing Luke, and at the same time, she was confused and hurt by the way Winter was acting. Her brother, Garrett, who followed her up the stairs, stopped her at the top. Surprised, she asked, "Hey, Garrett, what's wrong?" He rubbed his face in his hands before answering.

"I am worried about Winter. I like Luke, but I don't like the fancy talker. Win seems to act more and more like Spring every time I see her." Autumn smiled. "Jacob's okay. Luke has known him most of his life, and they're both good Christians." Garrett shook his head.

"Autumn, did you see them kiss tonight? When Luke kissed you, it was polite. Winter was making out with him! On the front porch! In front of everyone!" Autumn blushed at her brother's reference to Luke's kiss, and she did remember how Winter and Jacob acted.

"Well, Luke and I have only kissed one other time. Winter and Jacob has probably kissed many more times than that. But you're right. I'll talk to her." At that, her brother's face relaxed. "Thanks. Maybe she'll listen to you better." Autumn continued her way to bed and dreamt about Luke's kiss.

Spring's heart felt sick. She watched Luke kiss Autumn, and jealousy filled her. As far as she could remember, she had never been kissed like that. Never been kissed with… with… respect. The word shocked her, but it hit home. The truth hurt. All the guys that she dated treated her like trash. She looked over at Winter and Jacob. He kissed her passionately, pressing her up against the house, but his hands never tried to wander like the hands she knew of. Jacob's hands stayed at his side, intertwined with Winter's.

Her brother interrupted her thoughts.

"Dad, could you please make the fancy talker remove his tongue from my sister's face?"

Kent raised his eyebrows and looked out the window. Spring shut everyone out, trying to get the dirty feeling to leave. Once her sisters came inside, she found it hard to ignore the argument that erupted. Eventually, she went upstairs to shower, no longer able to stand feeling so filthy.

CHAPTER 11

Luke rolled over in bed and cracked an eye open. For a moment, he couldn't figure out where he was. *Oh yeah, it's Christmas morning, and I'm at my parents' house.* He groaned as dread washed over him, and he tried to make himself go back to sleep. But it was no use. It was his normal wake-up time, and he could hear his mother working in the kitchen. He stretched and made his way out of his parents' spare bedroom. His mother turned toward him as he entered the room.

"Good morning, sweetie. Sorry if I woke you." He smiled. "No, Mom, you didn't wake me. I usually get up at this time." She glanced at the clock, and it read five fifteen. She smiled and shook her head.

"I don't know what to do about you early risers! To be honest, it's hard for me to get up this early." He smiled at her again as he reached for the coffee. *She seems to be in a good mood. Maybe Christmas won't be so bad after all.* About that time, she turned and grabbed his arm, making him spill coffee on the counter.

"You don't have anywhere to go today, do ya?" He stared at his mother's serious face and hesitantly answered her, "No. Why?" Her face softened as she let go of his arm and smiled.

"Oh good! I just wondered because I know that you and Jacob have girls that live in these parts, and he left out just a while ago to see her, and I figured you might too." Luke choked on his coffee.

"What?" He looked at his watch just to double check the time.

"He's going to visit her this early?" He shook his head and groaned. His mother just patted his back and said, "Don't worry about him. At least you are doing the right thing." He turned to his mother. He couldn't believe she said that. He watched her for a while and decided that she had become even more snobbish than she was before.

Eventually, his dad and Izzy made it downstairs to the kitchen. When Izzy saw him, she ran and jumped into his arms.

"Luke! You came! You have no idea how much I have missed you!"

He laughed and hugged her back. "I've missed you too! This summer, you need to come out to the ranch again." She smiled at him. "I would love that!!" Their mother changed the subject as everyone sat down for breakfast.

"So, Luke, when are we going to meet this girl of yours?" Dread came over him, but he answered her anyway.

"I was thinking I would bring her out tomorrow if it's okay with you."

"Oh, of course! Of course, I would love to meet her." About that time, the phone rang, and Luke, being the closest one to it, answered, "Hello? Oh, hi, Sam, how's it—No! You tell Mom." Their mom looked up and grimly said, "Put him on speaker." Luke grudgingly did as he was told. The room was tense and silent as his brother's voice echoed across the room.

"Hey, Mom, I just called to let you know that we will be there around three o'clock this afternoon." The room fell silent again.

"But you said that you were going to spend Christmas with us this year."

"No, Mom, I said that we were going to spend Christmas morning with her folks and the evening with you." She slammed down her fork.

"You said something like that last year and ended up staying with her folks. You're always visiting them! I think you should tell your wife that your family counts too!" Luke put his face in his hands and thought, *Here it goes again*.

"We were thirty minutes late, Mom! You can hardly say that we spent the day there! And my wife knows that you count, but I don't appreciate the way you talk about her, so if you can't be civil, we won't come at all!" His mom's face turned red.

"Fine! If you don't care about your family enough to visit them on Christmas, then fine! You'll regret it later!"

"Argh! Mom! I do care! We will be there by three to see everyone, but if you try to make a scene, we *will* leave!" The click of the phone filled the room with silence and also ruined any possible conversation during breakfast.

After that, the day was pretty much ruined. His mother remained in a bad mood, and the tense feeling lingered in the air. His father said nothing to him or anyone, like usual. He just watched TV or read an old newspaper. So most of the day, Luke and Izzy just sat and talked about how things were getting worse with their mother.

"Luke, thanks for letting me spend part of the summer at your place. It's not so bad during school time, but I think I would go crazy if I had to spend the whole summer stuck in the house with Mom!" Luke smiled. "No problem! Just hang in there, and I'll be there for you if you need me."

"I know. Thanks."

Luke looked over at his almost too skinny sister as the cool December breeze blew her blond hair. Her light green eyes had sorrow in them. His heart ached for her, but until she graduated this spring, there was not much he could do to help her.

CHAPTER 12

Autumn pitched a fork of hay over the stall to her horse. Her mind and heart was still confused about the conversation she had with Winter earlier this morning. She had tried to voice her concerns about how fast she was moving with Jacob, but all it did was make her mad. Winter had told her not to worry about her and that she knew the boundary line. Then before Autumn could say anything else, Winter smiled at her, asked her to do her chores for her, and then ran out the door to meet Jacob who had just pulled up. Christmas morning, she ran off with him too, and they didn't see her until that evening. In fact, Christmas itself wasn't like it usually was. Spring sat and moped all day. Winter was gone. And everyone else just wasn't sure what to do next.

Autumn shook her head, trying to clear it. Then she groaned. Her boots sunk a little in the mud, telling her that her brother hadn't been mucking the stalls regularly.

"Garrett, thanks for all the extra work." She muttered to herself as she leaned the shovel against one of the stalls. She paused a moment to zip up the old barn coat that she wore over her button-up flannel.

"I wish I could see you like this every morning. You're better than coffee," was the whisper in her ear. She jumped and turned to find herself in Luke's arms. After the initial shock, she giggled. "Don't scare me like that!"

An apologetic look came on his face. "I didn't really mean to. Why don't you dress like that more often?"

She raised an eyebrow. "What, in mud boots and raggy old barn clothes? Are you serious—" He cut her off by pulling her over to him and kissing her. She melted into him. Taking a deep breath, he let her go. A little embarrassed by his actions, he asked, "So how can I help?" Autumn smiled. "You already have… I mean, you can feed while I finish mucking the stalls that my helpful brother forgot to do." Luke grinned. "Okay."

After a little while, Luke paused. "I can't believe it!" Confused, Autumn turned to look at him. "What?"

"I can't believe that I am standing in a barn that houses a quarter horse, an Arabian, a fox trotter, and a paint all at once." Luke suddenly turned to look at her and winced.

"So, which one is yours?" Autumn laughed. "The quarter horse!" She reached over to pat her black filly.

"Oh good!" Luke replied with relief.

She raised an eyebrow at him. Noticing, Luke began to explain, "The smartest horse is a quarter horse." Autumn laughed again.

"No, I'm serious! Arabians are hot-blooded. Fox Trotters flighty, more air brained. And paints aren't no better." Autumn shook her head. "I do like quarter horses better, but I think you are a little racist in your opinion. I've seen some smart horses that were not quarter." Luke grinned and leaned in close.

"So have I, but they are few and far between." Autumn shook her head at him, again smiling, and they went back to work. After they finished Lori had hot chocolate waiting for them.

"So, what do you two have planned for today?" Lori asked as she poured a cup of hot chocolate for herself.

"Well I thought I would take Autumn to meet my folks if it okay with you." Luke replied. Lori smiled and nodded.

"Yes, that will be fine. You two have fun and if you come back by six I'll have supper ready." Autumn and Luke finished their drinks then headed for the truck.

When Autumn and Luke pulled into his parents' drive, Luke's mother, Lisa, met them at the door.

"Oh, it is so nice to finally meet the girl that brought my boy back home!" Lisa gave her a hug that was a little awkward. Autumn gave a little smile. "Um… Pardon me.

What do you mean about me bringing him home?" Lisa smiled and led her to the table where Luke's dad, James, sat with a cup of coffee. He nodded a hello and smiled in her direction. Lisa's face got serious.

"Oh, Luke didn't tell you? I guess I shouldn't be surprised. Luke ran away from home. He's a stubborn thing, you know! Anyway, this is the first time he has come home for Christmas in a long while! So are you an orphan?" The question caught her by surprise.

"Um... No, I—"

"How is your relationship with your folks?" Autumn, feeling a little uncomfortable, forced a smile on her face.

"We have a good relationship." Lisa's face fell just a little with disappointment before she turned to the counter.

"So are you going to let my Luke come and see me very often? Or will I have to lose another son?" Before Autumn could answer, Luke's sister, Izzy, bounded into the room.

"Oh, wow! You are just as pretty as Luke described! I'm Izzy!" She held out her hand to a blushing Autumn. Autumn shook it, smiled and replied. "Nice to meet you. I hear we are a lot alike." Izzy sat down at the table and proceeded to get to know her new friend.

After a while, James's pager beeped at him. Autumn got an eerie feeling as the room immediately fell silent. He glanced at the screen and ran his fingers through his brown hair. Slowly, he stood up and walked over to his wife, Lisa, and gave a smile.

"Sorry, love, but I have to go deliver a baby." Lisa started to shake her head, obviously upset.

"James, this is the day after Christmas! Baby's take a while to get here anyway! Just call them back and tell them you can't come in." He reached up and tucked some of her blond hair behind her ear as his tired, blue eyes pleaded with her silently to not make a scene. Autumn saw him kiss her just before Luke and Izzy led her out the door.

Once outside, the mood lightened as Luke and Izzy showed Autumn around. It was a small farm with a handful of sheep. There wasn't much to show on the place, so they mostly just walked around and talked.

"I do have to agree with you, Luke. Cows do smell better than sheep." Autumn commented as she wrinkled her nose. He smiled as Lisa's sheep ran around the pen like a bunch of loons. A car coming up the drive caught his attention. "Oh, there's Sam. I'll introduce you." So they headed for the house and followed Sam and his wife, Ellie, through the front door.

"Sam, I am so happy to get to see you two days in a row!" Lisa said as she gave him a big hug.

"Ellie" was all she said to her son's wife. The red-haired beauty that stood beside Sam gave her the same acknowledgment.

"Lisa."

Ignoring her, Lisa led her oldest son to the table. "Here, honey, let me get you something to eat. You look like you could blow away! Is she not feeding you good enough?"

He let out a sigh. "Ellie feeds me good, sometimes too well." He smiled and threw a wink in his wife's direction.

"Anyway, Mom, I just need to borrow some of Dad's tools. Is he home?" Lisa, who had noticed the flirting between Sam and his wife, got a little snappy.

"No! He's not home. He had to go to work. But you should eat anyway. Her food apparently doesn't agree with you," Ellie snickered.

"He eats better now than he ever has with you." Said Ellie as she crossed her arms in front of her chest.

At that point, Luke jumped in. "Hey, everyone, I've got to get Autumn home, so we'll talk to you later."

Sam stood up and gave Luke a hug. "Well, it's nice to see you again! Stop by the house before you leave. Maybe drink some tea or something."

Luke smiled. "I'll do that." Sam shook Autumn's hand. "And nice to meet you." She smiled. "And nice to meet both of you." Autumn said in return. Ellie smiled back, shaking her hand. They finished with good-byes and headed to the truck.

Now she was in Luke's truck, letting her mind run through the day's events. But with his arm around her, she found it hard to think of anything else besides him. Luke gave her a little squeeze as he parked his truck in front of her house.

"Well, you've met my whole miserable bunch." Luke announced. Autumn gave him a little smile. "Your family isn't really that bad. Actually, it seems like my family is getting to be just as bad as you claim yours is." Luke let out a sigh. "I guess all we can do is pray." There was a little pause before Autumn said, "Your mom and Ellie don't get along very well, do they?"

Luke shook his head. "No. No, they don't. I think Mom feels like Ellie took or is trying to take her little boy away. You see, Sam was a mama's boy when he was younger. They did a lot together. She just doesn't want to realize that he is a grown man and she needs to let him go to have a family of his own." Autumn nodded in agreement. Luke kept talking, "In fact, I'm not sure what's going to happen when Izzy leaves home."

A tap on the window made them both jump. They had been so wrapped up in their discussion that they didn't notice Garrett walking toward them. Garrett opened the truck door and leaned against it.

"Care to join us for supper, or shall I tell everyone that you want to sit and talk out here until you freeze to death?" Autumn smiled at her brother and started to laugh. She reached over Luke and yanked on Garrett's ear-length black hair.

"I think I'll freeze, little brother. That is until you learn how to muck stalls and cut your hair!" This started a little sibling play fight that caused Luke to slide out of the truck in order to get out of the way. Kent and Lori, who had been watching from the window, came to the door.

"Luke, just leave them be and come on in. They'll join us when they get hungry enough." Luke chuckled a little to himself and walked toward the house.

CHAPTER 13

Spring didn't stay the whole Christmas vacation at Kent and Lori's. In fact, she left pretty soon after Luke had come to pick Autumn up to meet his family. She couldn't stand all of the happiness and everyone nagging her about her life. So with the excuse of work, she left early. As she pulled into the almost-empty college parking lot, her phone rang. It was Erik, and she smiled for the first time in hours.

"Hey, Erik, guess what? I am at the college! I couldn't stand being home any longer! Do you want to go somewhere?" The silence on the other end was like a slow-moving dagger into her heart. "Erik?"

"Yeah, Spree, I don't think this is going to work out. Keith's right. You're a fun ride, but I'm looking for a girl who isn't so easy, and I met one the other—" Spring hung up on him, and the onslaught of tears pushed at the back of her eyes as she realized that both men had played her. She had to leave, move, and do something. She found a little spot on campus that was private enough to suit her and let the tears erupt. Her body shook as all the pain and stress from the past few years flooded through her. *This wasn't how it was supposed to work! I was using them, I thought! I hate my life. Why do I even try to be happy? I should just give up and off myself! No one cares anyway. Everyone just thinks I'm a—*

Suddenly, a hand on her back made her jump. She turned around and realized that it was just her science lab partner.

"What do you want, Chad?" He awkwardly shuffled a little and tousled his red wavy hair. "I just saw that you looked upset, and I followed you to make sure you were okay." She shook her head and rested it against her knees. Chad had openly admitted his crush on her since the first day of college, and the crush deepened after his best friend Nathan started dating Summer.

She felt him sit down beside her. "Do… do you want to talk about it?" He asked.

She sneered at him. "No! Not with you or any other person of the male gender! All you want is sex, and when you tire, you find another. You're all rotten and deserve to be locked up!" She let out a string of curses as she put her head back down on her knees and heard him take a long breath.

"Spree, I am not like that. I could never be that way, especially to the woman I love."

She chuckled in a scary kind of way. "Oh, like I haven't heard that one before! What? Are you in with Keith and

Erik's little bet to see how many guys can sleep with me in one semester? You don't love me. You just want my body!" Chad tensed up, and a look that she had never seen before came on his face.

"No! I love you, and I wouldn't care if I never got anything from you. And for your information, I have taken a Christian vow to stay sexually pure until marriage. So I don't want it. I just want to care for you and show you how wonderful you are! I want to be there for you!" She started to sob again, and he put his arm around her.

"Just give me a chance." She sighed, stood up, and turned away from him.

"Fine, but just to warn you, I could leave you at any minute."

He took her hand. "Okay" was all he said as he wiped the tears from her eyes.

CHAPTER 14

The months had flown by for Autumn. Her and Luke had gotten closer and she yearned to be with him more. It was getting harder and harder to control fleshy urges. But Luke, who also wanted to remain pure until marrage, seemed to know when to step away. Luckily, school took up most of her time, keeping her away from Luke and temptation. Time went by quickly for the both of them. And now she was getting ready for spring break. She had just finished packing when her phone rang.

"Hey, Luke!"

"Howdy. I'm ready whenever you are." His deep voice rumbled through the phone. Autumn smiled. "Okay. I'm on my way." Autumn grabbed her bag and headed for her car. Luke wasn't able to come with her to Hickory this time, so he asked her to come over to his house before she left so he could give her a surprise.

When she got to his house, he was waiting for her with two already-saddled horses. He sauntered over and opened her door. His smile was breathtaking, and his eyes had a mysterious twinkle. She smiled back at him, and they embraced.

"Autumn, I've missed you." She stood up on her tiptoes and gave him a kiss. "I've missed you too. Can't wait to be done with school!" He took a long look at her as an unanswered question pulled at his heart. He pushed it away and then led her to the horses.

"Ready to ride?"

She giggled. "Yes! I've been wanting to ride all week!" The joyous expression on her face sent a chill through him. He could easily get used to making this woman smile! And he could easily picture her riding beside him for the rest of his life.

Coming back to reality, he winked at her and kicked his horse up into a canter. He wasn't surprised that she easily caught up and pulled alongside of him. He smiled over at her and pulled his horse down to a walk. She laughed. "You don't have to stop! I was having fun!" His smile widened. "I could tell, but the trail gets a little rough up here. Don't want to risk injury to the horses." Autumn nodded in understanding. She also couldn't imagine a more perfect way to spend the evening with Luke.

She turned to look at him. Even though he never talked a lot, the way he looked at her, as if trying to memorize her face, made her nervous heart skip. And the way he looked when he was cantering the horse made her lose even more concentration. If she had to find her way back to the house, she would be doomed because she had no clue where they were.

They finally made it to a little clearing where a little waterfall cascaded across the rocks of the creek bed. Luke tied up their horses and then went to spread a blanket over the tender spring grass. She helped him set up the picnic dinner that he had packed.

"Oh, Luke! This is beautiful!"

He smiled. "I hoped that you would like it." He dished out the food, hoping that she wouldn't care that it was just sandwiches. And of course, she didn't mind at all.

After they ate, Autumn leaned against him and watched the water run across the rocks. Luke, who was leaned up against a boulder, started to play with her long, silky, black hair. Luke wondered if she had any idea how hard it was for him to abstain from sexual sin. How hard it was to keep from crossing the line with her. Sometimes when they kissed the feeling became so overwhelming that he had to walk away from her to clear his head. He knew from earlier conversation that she wanted to wait till after marriage to have sex. He wanted the same thing. Waiting to have sex until after marriage was how God had intended it to be. And Luke wanted to obey God's word. But temptation warred with him constantly when he was with her and he found himself asking God for help several times. Luke knew that God wouldn't let him be tempted more than he could handle. But it was hard. So Luke found that time away from each other physically was best. That is why he declined Autumn's offer to go with her family to Florida. He needed time alone to do some serious praying about their relationship anyway. He studied her face. She was beautiful and she had a loving heart. *I cannot disgrace her honor God. Please give me the strength to keep her pure.* Luke closed his eyes and sighed when he ended the prayer. They both had been silent for some time. A question that had been on his mind lately beat against his brain. *No! I can't ask her that. At least not right now.* So instead he asked a different question.

"So, Autumn, what do you want out of life?" Autumn frowned. "What do you mean?"

"Where do you see yourself in five years? A fancy job, a family, twenty-seven cats?" Autumn burst into laughter.

"Twenty-seven cats! Are you serious? I don't really like cats!" Luke chuckled. Autumn sighed. "Well, I guess what I want the most is to have a family and be able to stay home with the kids. Maybe homeschool so the kids could have strong Christian roots before they are sent out into the world. But as for five years, I don't know where I will be or where God will put me. How about you?"

Luke was silent for a while before he said, "I would like to have a family by then." They both stayed quiet as he kept running his fingers through her hair. She closed her eyes and sighed. Luke watched her for a while and then very gently, tilted her face up so she would look at him.

"Autumn, I love you."

Her breath caught as she processed what he had just said. "I love you too, Luke." Autumn loved hearing him say that, but it took her by surprise every time.

A few days later, Winter walked hand in hand with Jacob as they walked along the creek that ran across the few acres that he had bought from Luke. The water splashed and trickled over the rocks, and the cows mooed softly as they ate at the gently swaying grasses. Winter's curly blond hair danced in the breeze, and Jacob's heart raced at the sight of it. But it didn't matter. She always took his breath away.

She laughed at something he had said. Her smile was radiant, and her butterscotch eyes sparkled. He could no longer resist. He pulled her into his arms and kissed her.

"I love you," he whispered into her ear. She giggled. "I love you too." He pulled her away to look at her. He could never hide behind fancy talk when she was around, so he always found it hard to speak.

"Winter, you know how I've been practicing a lot lately for the rodeo." Winter smiled. "Yes." Jacob took a breath. "Well, I have to leave out on the circuit next week." Silence fell between them.

"Winter, I can't leave you and not be able to see you for months on end." He took her hands and dropped down on one knee.

"Winter, I love you so much that I can't even imagine anyone better to stay by my side. Life on the road might not be the ideal honeymoon, but if you wish that I stay home next year, I will. Will... will you marry me?" Winter took a breath but remained silent. Jacob's heart kicked up a notch.

"I... I know it's short notice, but you once told me that you didn't want a big wedding. If you still feel this way, then we can go to the preacher tonight, and then we can have the reception with your family later." Winter just looked at him. This made his breath quicken.

"Uh... Winter, could... could you say somethin'?" Winter ran her fingers through his hair and let it rest on his cheek.

"Jacob, I love you, and I would love to marry you, but how sure are you that this is what God wants? Are we supposed to be together this soon?"

Jacob stood. "I have been praying for God to lead me to the right woman, and I have never received an answer or dated until you. I have felt attraction to other women, even spent some time in a group with them. But I have never had such a strong connection with anyone like I have with you. I have no doubt, just peace for this situation." Jacob couldn't look at her. He had never been this nervous before, not even in all those years of riding bulls. He felt

Seasons of Life

her hand touch his face again, and he closed his eyes. Her lips brushed his, and he kissed her back, not knowing what she meant by it. Did kissing him mean yes, or was this a kiss good-bye? After their lips parted, he looked into the concerned face of his only love and waited for her answer.

CHAPTER 15

Autumn almost danced into her dorm building. She had a pretty good spring break. After spending the evening with Luke, she went home to spend time with her family. Her family had always had a tradition of going to Florida for spring break just so they could get away from everyday life. It was a time to relax and just have fun. It was almost just like old times. Even Spring almost seemed to be like her old self. The only thing missing was Winter who hadn't informed anyone why she wasn't coming.

Autumn opened the door of her dorm, and she slid to a stop, the smile slipping off her face. Winter looked up at her but continued to pack her stuff.

"Wi… Winter, what are you doing?" Winter stopped and looked at her. She smiled. "Autumn, Jacob and I eloped yesterday. So I am packing to leave with him on the rodeo circuit." Autumn sat down in a chair. "Wha… what?"

Winter didn't turn to look at her. "I've already dropped out of my classes and signed all of the paperwork. Sorry I didn't call you, but I didn't want to interrupt your visit, and we haven't told anyone except Luke."

Autumn took a deep breath. "Well, don't you think you guys jumped the broom a little too quickly?"

Winter looked her straight in the eye. "If Luke had asked you, what would you have said?" Autumn opened her mouth but couldn't speak. She didn't know what to say. Winter nodded. "That's what I thought." Autumn's eyes started to tear up a bit as she walked over and hugged her.

"Sorry. Congratulations. I hope you two will be happy."

Winter smiled. "Thanks. Um… could you call Kent and Lori for me later?"

Autumn nodded. "Yeah, I will but I'm not sure how happy they will be."

Autumn helped Winter finish packing and listened to her tell her how it happened. Autumn still found it hard to grasp the fact of her sister being married. *It happened so fast. I had no idea that their relationship had reached that point.* Autumn started to wonder if maybe Winter was making a mistake. *But what could I say? What's done is done. Winter and Jacob are now bound together for life. And Winter is right. If Luke had asked me I would have said yes.* Autumn pushed the thoughts from her mind and tried to concentrate on what Winter was saying. After Autumn helped Winter carry her stuff to the parking lot, Autumn hugged her good-bye and watched her leave. Autumn stood there for a minute, unsure of what to do. The cool spring breeze chilled her. Then she remembered that Luke had asked her to come over when she got back in town. She was already late, so she numbly climbed into her car and left.

Luke wasn't surprised that Autumn was late. He pitched another fork of hay over the fence to his horses before he went over to her car. She hugged him. Oh, how he had missed her. Talking on the phone hadn't helped his longing to see her. He kept holding her, noticing that she was in no hurry to leave his arms.

"Sorry I'm late. I was helping Winter pack. Is that why you wanted me to come over, to tell me they eloped?" Luke stroked her hair. "No, actually I had already planned and invited you before I found out." He felt her relax. "I've missed you," he whispered into her ear.

"I've missed you too." She replied.

He felt her tighten her grip on him. He rubbed her back. "Hey, I have a surprise for you."

She looked up at him and smiled. "I love you. You always seem to make me feel better!"

He kissed her and told her that he loved her as well. Then he took her by the hand and led her toward the house. Luke washed up and started to cook. His kitchen was small but tidy. Out of habit, Autumn went to help.

Seasons of Life

"So, Autumn, How was Florida?" Luke asked as he seasoned the steaks. Autumn continued to slice onions as she spoke, "It was fun actually. Spring seems happier than she has been. She acted like she enjoyed herself! It seemed like old times aside from no one not being able to get a hold of Winter." Luke watched Autumn for a second before asking, "So what all did you do?"

"Well we swam of course! Oh! Me, Garret, Summer, and Spring did spend an entire day building an enormous sandcastle that was almost as tall as you. We were so tired that night that we ended up falling asleep on the couch!" Luke laughed at that.

"That is something I would liked to have seen!" Luke said. Autumn smiled.

"Oh, don't worry! I did manage to get a picture of it before Spring and Garret destroyed it." Autumn shook her head at the memory. Luke turned to her and asked, "Why did they destroy it?" Autumn giggled.

"Well they didn't mean to. You see, We had just finished taking pictures of it and Garret suggested that we dig a moat around it to keep the ocean from washing it away. Well, after a short time of working on it, Garret accidentally threw a bucket of sand on Spring. After yelling at him about it she scooped some sand in her bucket and flung it back at him! It started a war between all of us and kind of morphed into something along the lines of tag and wrestling! And long story short, Garret knocked Spring into a wall. Then

Spring returned the favor. After that it was a free-for-all and we all ended up knocking down some part of it! Mom actually was able to get some of it on tape."

At this point Luke was laughing so hard that tears were coming to his eyes. "No wonder you all were exhausted!" Luke said as he wiped the tears from his face.

"Yeah, it was nice to just goof off and laugh with each other again! If Winter had been there it would have been perfect." The smile slid from her face. "Well, I guess I had better go call mom and dad for Winter and tell them what's going on." Luke nodded as she left the room to make the call. When she came back in to the room she shook her head.

"They are not happy. They would've liked to have been there. I can kind or understand how they feel." Luke rubbed her shoulder to relieve the tension.

"Don't worry about it Autumn. It will all work out in the end. Praying to God about it will do the most good." Autumn smiled up at him.

"Yeah, your right. Thank you." Autumn gave Luke a small kiss and helped him finish cooking.

When the food was done and grace was said, they continued to talk on and off about different topics. Autumn sighed, "This is nice." Luke smiled. "The food? Or being with me?" She laughed. "Both! I like eating and I love the company."

Luke smiled at her as he cleared his throat. "So I was thinking. How would you like to run a house of your own?

I could get used to this, being with you." He paused for a second, and then he took her hand and got down on one knee.

"Autumn, will you walk with me for the rest of my life? Will you marry me and be my wife?" He pulled a little gold band with a small diamond on it out of his pocket. A smile erupted on her face. "Yes! Of course!"

He slid the ring onto her finger, and she leaped into his arms, knocking him to the floor. They laughed and he kissed her. "I almost didn't ask you 'cause I didn't want you to think I was asking because of Jacob. I seriously did plan this before you left for spring break." Autumn leaned against the cabinet and smiled.

"I believe you! So when were you planning on us getting hitched?" She asked.

Luke sat beside her and intertwined their fingers. "I was thinking maybe in September. You say it's your favorite month, and it should give us plenty of time to plan. You will also be finished with college. And the house still needs a few things to be ready for a woman. But if you want to elope like our friends did, I'm okay with that too."

Autumn smiled. "No, I think September is just fine. I don't want to be a copycat, and I am sure our families would like to be there."

He smiled back at her. "Okay. September it is."

CHAPTER 16

Autumn ran her hand down her white satin dress as she looked at herself in the mirror. Her hair laid across her back in black ringlets with just enough hair pinned back to hold up her veil. Butterflies danced in her stomach for she was nervous and excited at the same time. The thought of her starting the next chaper of her life, made her light headed. And she couldn't believe that this day had finally come.

"You look so beautiful!" Summer said as she bounced over to touch one of her curls.

"Yeah, thanks for *not* helping me go through the time-consuming process of trying to get all of those curls to stay!" Spring replied as she slapped at Summer's hand, then turned to packed up her hair products. Winter rolled her eyes at her two sisters.

Summer raised an eyebrow. "I was busy." Autumn smiled at her sisters. She was so glad when she found out that they

Seasons of Life

all could make it to be her bridesmaids. A knock sounded on the door.

"Who is it?" Summer asked.

"It's me. Luke." All three of Autumn's sisters run to the door to keep him out. " I know I'm not supposed to see you until later, but if I could, I would like to pray with you before the ceremony." The room was silent for a second.

"I would like that as well. I'm glad you thought of it." Autumn's sisters still insisted that he should not see her, so they cracked the door open enough so that they could hold each other's hands. Luke's deep voice rumbled as he began to talk to their savior.

"Father God, we come before you today to ask you to bless our marriage and the beginning of our lifelong vow to each other and to you. I know that there will be hard times, and I ask that you will help us through those times, Lord. And please let our marriage be a witness for you and show the world how amazing you truly are. Thank you for bringing us together. You are truly the master matchmaker! And we will forever serve you. In Jesus's name, amen!" Autumn squeezed his hand as she gave her "amen." Spring, who was feeling uncomfortable, replied, "Okay! Now that, that is done, I will fix your tear-streaked makeup, and we'll get this show on the road!" Luke left to tell the preacher that they were ready, and the music started to play. With a smile the girls, hurried to take their places.

Luke glanced around the ranch yard, it was covered with red, orange, and yellow. Square hay bales served as chairs, and the grapevine archway was set up under a giant red maple. Kerosene lanterns hung from the trees and all the tables were lain with a white table cloth adorned with red, orange, and yellow leaves. It was beautiful.

When the wedding started everyone fell silent as the wedding party entered one by one. Finally Autumn stepped out of the house, crossed the deck, and made her way toward Luke. He caught his breath at the sight of her. A smile spread across his face as he took her hand from Kent's (unfortunately, her real dad, Frank, wasn't able to come). Luke really wanted to hold her in his arms and kiss her, but he restrained himself. His hands trembled as he slid the tiny gold band onto her delicate finger. He didn't know how long he could control himself from kissing her. Fortunately for Luke, the wedding wasn't long, and he was soon able to kiss his bride, and they were pronounced husband and wife. The crowd of family and friends cheered (well, most hollered, shouted, or sent out a whistle—mainly the cowboys). After the cake and food was served, the fun show started. Hoof beats sounded as one game followed another, and the sound of children laughing was constant. Luke smiled at his new bride. This would defiantly be a day that they would remember.

CHAPTER 17

Paul moseyed over to Summer, who he had met for the first time at the rehearsal dinner. Autumn and Summer looked enough alike to be twins, but in Paul's opinion, Summer was far prettier. Her bright blue eyes would shine and seem to make her hair shimmer but when turned on him, would pierce his heart, making him feel something he never had before. Summer had already changed out of the bridesmaid's dress and was leaning against a tree when Paul walked up behind her and scared her.

"Paul, don't do that!"

Paul smiled and leaned up against the tree that she had abandoned. "I said it before, and I'll say it again. You are gorgeous!"

Summer couldn't help but smile. "Yes, and I told you I was seeing someone."

He smiled. "Then where is he?" She shook her head. "Not that it is any of your business, but anyway, he couldn't make it."

He ignored her answer and almost got lost in her smile. "Well, walking you down the aisle today, I couldn't help but think"—he leaned closer to her, so close her heart fluttered, and he whispered—"that I was the luckiest man on earth to be able to hold the only woman who was prettier than the bride." Summer, who was starting to feel guilty for being that close to another man besides Nathan and liking it, rolled her eyes at him and pushed him back. "You're a charmer!" She walked away, smiling, unable to hide that she was pleased by his comment. But inwardly, she willed herself to forget the way he made her feel. Paul watched her walk off, taking in her every move. Still smiling, he finally pushed himself off the tree and went to go get his horse ready.

Luke, on the other hand, couldn't take his eyes off his new wife. Her beauty was breathtaking, and instead of staying for the whole fun show, he decided to whisk her away to their honeymoon destination. As they drove off to the sound of loved ones honking their car horns, they kissed, unable to believe that they finally belonged to each other, and happiness showed from their faces like the sun that set the clouds ablaze before them.

CHAPTER 18

Jacob wrapped his arms around his wife and kissed her. "I love you!" he whispered into her ear. She giggled. "I love you too!" With that, he kissed her once more before climbing through the fence to join the other bull riders. This was going to be his last ride for the season before he settled down for the first winter with his wife. Winter sat down with Autumn, who had come to watch her husband, Luke, and his partner, Paul, rope. They watched one man after another ride until Jacob's turn came. He sat on the bull and slid his hand under the bull rope while another cowboy tied on the flanking strap. The bull lurched in the shute, making the other cowboys who were helping him get ready, jump back to keep from getting their hands and arms crushed between the massive animal and its cage. Finally, Jacob gave his nod. The gate flew open, and the timer was started. He rode gracefully, matching the bull move for move, but just before the eight-second buzzer sounded, the bull jerked sharply to the left and kicked it's back feet. Throwing Jacob off balance, and off of the bull. But his hand stuck in the ropes, leaving his body to dangle dangerously at the beast's side. The bull continued to buck again and again, barely missing Jacob's abdomen but sometimes catching his foot or a leg. Fear pulsed through him as he fought against the ropes. Adrenalin coursed through his body causing sweat to run down his face. The crowd gasped in horror, and a panicked scream pierced the air. "Jacob!" His hand finally gave way as a rodeo clown scrambled to help get the ropes loose. He fell to the ground as the bull's hind foot clipped his rib cage. He lay there motionless as shooting pain rendered him frozen. He knew he had to get out of the arena. He heard people running toward him. But before help reached him, the hatred-filled bull dodged the men on horseback and headed back for Jacob. Its horns pierced his upper arm, which he had thrown up to defend himself. But he wasn't able to avoid the hoof that caught him right below the shoulder, crushing several ribs. The rodeo clowns and men on horseback raced toward the bull, turning it away from the motionless body that lay limp on the ground.

When Winter finally made her way to him, paramedics were pulling into the arena.

Seasons of Life

"Jacob! Jacob, please!" She sobbed as she cradled his head out of the puddle of blood.

"Jacob," she whispered.

"Get her out of here!" one of the paramedics shouted. Luke's strong grip pulled her away as a paramedic's hands replaced hers. A soft moan from her love sounded as Luke took her.

"No!" she screamed.

"Let me go back! I need to be with him! Let me go!" She fought with all her might, tears streaming down her face like a hard rain. Finally, Luke gripped her hard on her shoulders and shook her.

"Winter stop! He needs professional help right now! And God's help even more! So if you want to help, then pray." She gasped, finally silent, noticing for the first time that her captor had tears running down his face too. She straightened up and walked quickly by his side.

"Take me to the hospital?" Her voice was still shaky, so it came out as a whisper. Luke turned to Paul who was, at the moment, standing by a very white-faced Autumn.

"Paul, will you take Winter to the hospital? I need to attend to my wife." Paul nodded in understanding as he put an arm around Winter to comfort her. Luke prayed that neither of the women would have nightmares after this. He knew all too well what something like that could do to one's head. Paul helped Winter into his truck, unhooked his horse trailer, and drove off. Winter started to cry, so Paul patted her shoulder.

"Hey, it will be okay. Whatever God's plan is will be for the best." He said. She nodded but still cried, only softer.

CHAPTER 19

A week later, Winter sat by her husband's side, watching his unconscious face. The doctors had done all that they could in fixing him, but with the massive blood loss and several ribs shattered, he hadn't woke up. She gently caressed his cheek, memorizing his face, and since she was alone with him, she bent down and kissed him lightly.

"I love you," she whispered as a single tear rolled down her cheek. She held his hand in hers while she prayed. Then she laid her head on the bed, willing herself not to cry, but a slight tug on one of her curls made her lift it again. Jacob's eyes lay upon her.

"Oh, Jacob!" She hit the call button and informed the staff that he had woke.

"Winter," he whispered so softly, she could barely hear. So she sat on the edge of the bed and leaned closer.

"I can't stay…" came his weak words.

"Jac—"

"Shh... thank you for making my life amazing. Thank you for being a part of my life."

Tears started to fall from her eyes. He kept talking. "I know you'll take good care for our little girl."

Winter's mouth fell open. "Wha—"

"She's beautiful just like you."

Her heart felt like it was ripped in two and she started to cry harder. "But, Jake, I need you here!" Jacob slowly raised his hand to touch her face. Pain evident on his face. He struggled to take his next breath. The doctor walked in just as a strangled "I love you" fell from his lips and his eyes fell shut. His heart monitor sounded the alarm when his heart stopped. The doctors and the nurses tried to save him, but he was unresponsive. After the staff called the time of death, Winter clung to his body and cried until Kent led her away.

A few hours later, Spring bounced into the waiting room where the rest of her family sat comforting Winter.

"Hey guys! Sorry I'm late. I had my phone off, so what's going on?" They all stared at her, but before anyone could answer, she kept talking. "Wow! You all look like you're going to a funeral."

Summer stood up. "You are horrible! And selfish! All you think about is yourself! And hooking up with some guy!" She pushed past Spring and walked out. Spring stood there, shocked. She looked at everyone in the room. No one said a thing. Tears swelled up in her eyes, but anger replaced the hurt as she pushed the tears back. "Some family! You claimed that I would have a real family if I let you adopt me, but clearly, you lied!"

Kent stepped forward. "Spre—"

"No! Don't touch me!" She took a step back and pointed at everyone in the room.

"You all have no idea the horror I had to go through as a child! You all with your perfect lives! With your perfect relationships! Don't judge me!"

Winter, who had been facing the window the whole time, turned toward her. "Spree, in God's eyes, all sin is the same. The only thing different between you and me is that Jesus's blood covers my sin so God won't see it. But he can see yours. The only difference, Spree? With Jesus, I will go to heaven, but you, my dear sister, without some serious prayer to Jesus, will find yourself one day in hell." She turned back to the window, and the room was dead silent. An eerie chill went through Spring. It shook her so badly that all she could say came out in a whisper, "Don't judge me." And she left before the tears came.

As she made her way down the many corridors, Autumn ran up beside her.

"Don't apologize for her, Autumn!"

Autumn grabbed Spring's hand to stop her from walking any farther.

"I wasn't going to because she's right. I came to tell you that Jacob died from getting attacked by that bull. A piece if his rib that the doctor missed got lodged in his heart." Spring sucked in a breath, and Autumn continued. "The crazy thing is Jacob woke up before he died and said that she was going to have his daughter. Out of curiosity, the doctor had her take a test, and she's pregnant! Heaven and God is real—"

Spring shook her head. This was too much for her. "You lie! He's not dead! Liar!" She turned and ran away, leaving Autumn standing by herself. Spring bumped into her boyfriend, Chad, as she was coming out of the elevator.

"Hey, I heard Jacob died. Poor Winter."

She gave him a dirty look. "Take me way from here. You're done with school, so let's just go somewhere far way where no one knows us."

Chad looked at her carefully. "But what about your degree? You're not finished with it."

She grabbed him by the shirt. "Do you think I want to go back to a place where everyone sneers at me and calls me a slut all of the time? Please take me away!" She started to drag him to the door, but he stopped her.

"Spring, we can't just run off. That wouldn't be seen well if an unmarried couple run off. Plus, it wouldn't help us with temptation to abstain." She hung her head, vowing to never return to that family again and took a deep breath before she turned to look at him.

"Fine, I will marry you. Maybe not today or tomorrow or next week, but *if* you run away with me now, I will marry

Seasons of Life

you later." She turned on all of her charm, silently begging him as he looked into her pleading eyes. And his spirit and flesh warred. The battle against sin raged hotter when she reached up to kiss him. "Push her away," his spirit told him, but flesh told him to let her continue. With a sigh, he let his flesh win the fight as they kissed.

"Okay," he said as he looked at the woman who he thought loved him. And he let the monster called lust persuade him to follow her out the door.

Life is not easy. Everyone struggles with something in one way, shape, or form. As life runs its course, changes its tide, and one season flows into another, each of the four girls face trials ahead. How will Winter handle being a single mom? And will she ever let her heart heal in order to move on? Will Spring stop trying to tread the waters of life by herself and learn to lean into her creator for help? When tragedy strikes will Summer be able to over come personal struggle? And Autumn, can her and Luke keep their relationship strong when the world pushes in around them? As life changes its seasons, the saga its self continues.

ACKNOWLEDGMENT

I would like to think:

First of all, My God, for helping me through more trials than I can count.

My husband, who lovingly took care of the kids and cleaned the house on the days that I was on a writing rampage and was unable to still my hand. And for believing in me and giving me lots of encouragement.

My mom and grandma for believing in me and offering their encouragement.

My mother-in-law and grandmother-in-law, for taking time out of their day to read over my work and offering suggestions.

My church for their prayers and many other people in my life.